THOMAS McKEAN

AN AVON CAMELOT BOOK

AVON BOOKS, INC.
1350 Avenue of the Americas
New York, New York 10019

Copyright © 1997 by Thomas McKean
Published by arrangement with the author
Visit our website at http://www.AvonBooks.com
Library of Congress Catalog Card Number: 97-444
ISBN: 0-380-79082-3

First Avon Camelot Printing: December 1998
First Avon Books Hardcover Printing: December 1997

CAMELOT TRADEMARK REG. U.S. PAT. OFF. AND IN OTHER COUNTRIES, MARCA REGISTRADA, HECHO EN U.S.A.

Printed in the U.S.A.

OPM 10 9 8 7 6 5 4 3 2

For Mombo and Poppo

Wednesday, September 5, after school

I know this is going to turn into a real adventure. In fact, I'm sure of it. That's why I've decided to start this journal. I want to remember everything that happens.

And it's kind of funny, but I wouldn't be having this adventure if it weren't for my name.

Jellimiah John Jensen—that's me.

How could anyone ever name their kid Jellimiah? Well, that's what my mother named me. It was her father's name, and now it's my name, too. When people ask me my name I always say it's John. That's my middle name, after my father. I don't ever tell people about the Jellimiah part. But somehow it always slips out. And then I'm called Jelly or Jelly-Belly or Smelly-Jelly. I hate it. That's what happened in my old school. I was just plain John in first and second grade. But then, the first day of third grade, my teacher called me Jellimiah in front of the class. From then on it

1

was good-bye John, hello Smelly-Jelly. My mom calls me John 'cause I make her. But back at my old school, no one else did.

So you can bet I was glad when Mom announced we had to move from Los Angeles to some small town just north of New York City.

"I've been offered a position as chief surgeon in an excellent hospital," Mom explained. "I hate to uproot you . . ."

Good, I remember thinking as she kept on talking. *When I get to my new school, I'm not going to let anyone know about the Jellimiah bit. I'll be John again. No more dumb nicknames. It's worth crossing the continent to lose the Jellimiah.*

It was even decent timing. My school in Los Angeles was closing—redistricting or something. Seventh grade in a new school in a new state with a new name. It sounded pretty good to me.

I even talked the school secretary into retyping my official transcript. "Please take out the Jellimiah," I begged, "and send one with only the name John."

"You've been such a good kid," said the secretary. "And your mother *does* call you John."

Yes! I had done it! I spent the summer feeling pleased with myself.

This morning was my first day at Edgewood Junior High.

"I'm John Jensen and I'm new here," I said as I reported to the front office.

"Welcome to Edgewood," said a tall woman with an amazingly long nostrils and an even longer neck. As she led me into her office she introduced herself as Miss Thompson. She reminded me of a giraffe having a bad day. "As principal," she told me, "I always like to take a special interest in our new students."

She gave me a terrible smile and looked down at my transcript. She leafed through some pages and seemed to be frowning.

I wondered what she could she be frowning about. My grades were good, all B+'s and A's. I'm certainly not a troublemaker. In fact, sometimes I think I'm *too* good. Once in a while I try being bad. But somehow I can never carry it off. To tell the truth, I've always been a little too scared to get into much trouble anyway. I guess I'm not in the least like my grandfather. He was some kind of wild guy, or so says Mom. I've always wanted to be kind of a wild guy, too, but I just never seem to get the chance.

Anyway, Miss Thompson gave a sudden snort.

"Where is Jellimiah?" she said.

"Jellimiah?" I began, my heart sinking. "I was hoping—"

"Twins are so fascinating," interrupted Miss Thompson, and I realized she hadn't been frowning after all. That was just the way she looked. "Yes," she continued, "you and your brother, Jellimiah—such an unusual name!—will be the only set of twins in the seventh grade."

"But I don't have a twin—" I started.

Miss Thompson ignored me. "And you're both such good students, too. And so twinlike! Why, look at these two sets of transcripts! Except for the first name, they're identical! You both took exactly the same courses and received exactly the same grades! I bet you look exactly alike, too."

So the secretary had sent both transcripts by mistake. That's when the idea hit me. I was starting over. I could be anyone—or anything—I wanted. For once in my life, I would do something bad. I would become twins!

I didn't even think about it. I jumped right in.

"Yes," I told Miss Thompson, "we're completely, entirely,

and, um, absolutely identical. Even our mother can't tell us apart."

"How fascinating," said Miss Thompson. "But John," she asked, "where *is* Jellimiah?"

That's when my next idea hit me. Not only would I have a twin, I'd have an evil twin!

I bowed my head. I was trying not to smile, but it must have looked to Miss Thompson as though I were upset about something.

"John," she said in her piercing voice, "is something the matter? You can confide in me. In fact, I shall confide in you. I'll tell you something I've never told another student: I don't consider myself the principal. I consider myself the students' Very Best Friend."

I raised my head. I tried to look upset and in need of a Very Best Friend.

"Oh, Miss Thompson," I said, hardly believing I was saying all this, "it's my brother. He's . . . he's . . ."

"Yes?" cried Miss Thompson. "What is he?"

What *was* he?

"He's no good," I said simply. "He was the biggest troublemaker in California. And I do mean the biggest."

"Oh, my!" exclaimed Miss Thompson. "How troubling! No wonder you said you didn't have a twin."

"Yes," I agreed. "It's hard having a twin brother like that."

"I should think so," said Miss Thompson. "But where is he? Don't tell me he's skipping his very first day of school!"

"Oh, no," I said. "He's not skipping. He's . . . he's . . ."

"Yes?"

"He's still in reform school," I burst out. "He was there all summer. They've been trying to straighten him out."

"Reform school!" cried Miss Thompson. "I didn't think they still had reform schools!"

Whoops, I thought. Out loud I said, "Um, it was *like* a reform school. And Jellimiah always called it reform school."

"Hmm," considered Miss Thompson, "perhaps it was a remedial program of some sort. But it doesn't say anything in his transcript about being such a troublemaker."

"Um, he told our last principal that if he left all the bad stuff in, he'd get back at him. So the principal took it out."

"Well, I shall call right up and get the full story," vowed Miss Thompson.

"You can't," I said. "They closed our school. Los Angeles is a big place. I don't even know where they're storing our old records."

Miss Thompson shuffled through the transcripts, shaking her head. Then she looked up. "When will your brother be, ah, finished with his . . . his . . ."

"His reform school? He gets out tonight. And please, Miss Thompson, promise me you won't tell him I told you all this stuff."

"I promise," the principal said solemnly. "Just tell me—when will Jellimiah begin here at Edgewood Junior High?"

"Tomorrow," I replied. "He'll be here tomorrow. You'll meet him then."

"I can hardly wait," said Miss Thompson.

Thursday, September 6, first period

It's only first period and it's already been quite a day! It's a good thing I have study hall so I can write in my journal and think.

It all began this morning at seven-thirty. I was looking at myself in the mirror in the hall. I had a lot of work to do and very little time in which to do it.

"Have a nice day, dear," called Mom as she hurried off to the hospital.

"You too," I replied. Then I began scrutinizing my reflection all over again.

It's not that I'm bad-looking or anything. It's just that I'm kind of, well, boring. My blond hair is always neatly parted and combed just so. My shirts are always ironed and buttoned right to the top. My pants are creased and my shoes are shined. Mom says I look as though I'm going to an interview. I've always wanted to look a little different, a little wilder. But you know how it is—once you start acting one way, it's hard to change. At least it has been for me. Until now. Now is my big chance.

I decided I'm going to be different—really different.

I'm going to be noticed.

My evil twin is going to turn heads.

I certainly didn't turn heads on my own.

Like yesterday, my first day at Edgewood Junior High.

Mr. Sterling, the homeroom teacher, introduced me to the class. "I hope you'll welcome John Jensen, our new student from California."

I thought I noticed a spark of interest when the other kids heard I was from California. But I saw the spark go out when they looked at me. A pretty girl in the front row gave a big yawn. And a jock in the third row just shook his head. It's not hard to figure out by looking at me that I'm no major athlete.

A boring clod. That seemed to be their verdict.

And it didn't help in math class when I knew the right answer to every question. I can't help it if I'm smart.

A smart, boring clod.

I ate lunch by myself in the noisy cafeteria. No one asked me to sit with them. No one. I'd kind of thought that a small school like Edgewood would be friendlier. Well, it wasn't to me. I might as well have been the Invisible Man.

But I was going to change all that. That's what I decided this morning.

First I messed up my hair so it was standing on end. I added some of Mom's mousse stuff to make sure it stayed a mess. In my room I found the ratty clothes I wear when I'm doing yard work—an old pair of jeans and a work shirt so ancient that George Washington could have worn it when he crossed the Delaware. If he'd worn work shirts, that is. I ripped the jeans into shreds so they just barely held together. I looked as though I'd stumbled into a huge electric fan. Rummaging through my closet, I found a pair of black boots. They were a little big, but they stayed on, so that was okay. I think they used to be my father's. I wonder why he left them behind when he walked out on Mom and me. And I wonder why we brought them with us when we moved—it's not like I ever wore them before.

Anyway, I went back to the mirror.

I had to laugh out loud. I hardly recognized myself.

"Jellimiah, you dog," I said out loud to myself, "you're gonna knock 'em dead!"

I grabbed my—I mean John's!—homework and headed for school. Miss Thompson had told me—whoops again, I mean John—to escort me (Jellimiah, that is) to her office when I got to school.

Edgewood Junior High is a modern school. It has a number of different buildings, all connected by open-air walkways. It's built in the middle of some woods, too. And it's nice and small—the entire junior high population is less than the number of kids in one grade in my old school in L.A.

"So," said Miss Thompson, looking me up and down severely when I arrived in her office, "you are Jellimiah."

"Yeah," I said. "That's my name. Don't wear it out."

Miss Thompson snorted. "Jellimiah," she said, "you are in a new school now. You start with a clean slate. I advise you to make use of this opportunity."

"My plan exactly," I replied.

Miss Thompson gave another one of her terrible smiles. "You might consider following your brother's example."

"That dork?" I said. "Not in a million years."

Miss Thompson sighed so hard her nostrils quivered.

Then she tried looking sympathetic. "Jellimiah," she said, "starting a new school can be hard. But let me confide in you. I'll tell you something I've never told another student: I don't consider myself the principal. I consider myself the students' Very Best Friend."

"That's what you said—" I began, then stopped. I suddenly realized that being two people was going to be trickier than I'd imagined. I bet this journal will come in handy, just keeping track of things.

"Yes?" asked Miss Thompson, raising an eyebrow.

"Forget it," I mumbled, shaking my head.

"Jellimiah," she said after clearing her throat, "I can see you are an entirely different person from your brother John—entirely different. I don't just mean your clothing. I can see it in your eyes. And I am never wrong. Never."

I just raised my eyebrows and stared at her. Hard, too. That's something I'd never do as John.

Miss Thompson looked a bit nervous, kind of like a giraffe who feels something nibbling at its leg but doesn't know what it is.

"At any rate," she continued, "I trust your, ah, work over the summer taught you something."

"What do you mean, 'my work over the summer'?" I demanded.

"I believe your brother referred to it as reform school."

Can you believe it? She promised not to let on I told her.

"That jerk," I said out loud.

"Now, now—we'll have none of that. Here's your schedule of courses. For the moment you and your brother are in all the same classes. We don't normally put twins together, but we weren't aware you were twins until only recently. We'll probably make adjustments later on. I asked that dear brother of yours to show you around. Is he waiting outside?"

"That creep," I said, enjoying myself. "Nah. He's not in school today."

"Oh, my," said Miss Thompson. "Is he ill?"

"Nah," I said, "he's, um, he . . . yeah, that's it. He hurt his wrist. Badly, too."

"Oh, my!" she cried again. "How did it happen?"

I did my best to give sort of a nasty smirk. "I guess he fell down," I said.

A road map of wrinkles appeared on Miss Thompson's forehead. I could tell she was wondering if I had had something to do with it—just the way I wanted her to.

"But how?" Miss Thompson persisted.

I shrugged. "These things happen," I said, smirking again. (It was easier the second time.) "But he gave me his homework to hand in," I added, waving around my assignments.

"The dear boy," enthused Miss Thompson. "Let him be a model for you."

Leaving Miss Thompson still glaring at my shredded clothes and me, I headed for homeroom.

Mr. Sterling wasn't as happy to see me as he'd been to see John.

"Class," he said in a cold voice, "meet John's twin brother, Jellimiah Jensen."

"Jellimiah?" mocked a boy in the second row.

"You heard the man. Jellimiah," I repeated loudly and proudly. "That's my name. Make sure you say it right: Jel-li-mi-ah." Why haven't I been able to do that before?

This morning the pretty girl didn't yawn. I'd learned her name was Sondra Settle. Her eyes followed me all the way to my seat.

The jock still looked unimpressed, but I had that all figured out. His name is Ralph Wypikowski, but everyone calls him Whip. My seat is right near his.

"Hey," I said to him. "You got a football team here?"

"Of course," he said. "What's it to you?"

I gave another of my smirks. "What's it to me? I was L.A.'s third-rated quarterback."

"Wow," he said. "But you look kind of slim for football."

"I'm one hundred percent muscle," I said nonchalantly.

Whip looked impressed. "So will you be going out for the team? Tryouts are next week."

I shrugged. "Yeah. But I've got to wait till my ligament heals—I twisted my leg waterskiing."

"You waterski?"

"I'm triple-class-rated," I said, hoping Whip knew less about waterskiing than I do. I've never been on a pair of water skis in my life.

"Triple-class," said Whip, giving a low whistle. "Wow!"

I smiled. He *does* know less about waterskiing than I do.

"Jellimiah," barked out Mr. Sterling, "homeroom is a time to get ready for the day's work, not to chat. Your brother appeared to understand that. I suggest you—"

But he never got to make his suggestion.

The bell rang and the day began.

My first full day as the new, improved Jellimiah Jensen— my evil twin.

〰️

Thursday, September 6, after school

Bad. I'm going to be bad. And not just bad—I'm going to be *evil*.

That's what I decided as I left study hall this morning. I'm going to make Jellimiah into the most evil twin a twin ever had. But then what? Then after a few days I'll get rid of him. That won't be hard. And besides, by then Edgewood Junior High will be so glad to see him go, they won't care how or why he left. And in the meantime I'll get to do all the things I'd never do if I had to be me. I'm going to have fun. And I'm going to get into trouble. Lots of trouble.

The only problem is, I'm not exactly sure how to get into trouble. It's kind of outside my own personal experience.

But I think I can do it. I'm smart. And today I made a start.

There I was, thinking about trouble as I was sitting in Mr. Fishwell's science class today. I'd overheard all the bad news about him yesterday—how he's the meanest, most horrible teacher in the whole school. It was the last class before lunch, and I was just wondering if I'd be eating alone again. Then suddenly my first evil idea hit me like a ton of bricks.

Mr. Fishwell was droning on about how dangerous chemicals are—that same old lecture they always give us in science class. "Don't play with chemicals!"—as if I would anyway!

Mr. Fishwell is a big man with short red hair. Today was a warm day, and he was sweating all over. The science lab where we sat *was* pretty warm. But somehow Sondra Settle managed to look cool. Her long auburn hair was pulled back with a blue clip, and she had a dreamy look in her eyes. I could tell she wasn't thinking about chemicals or Mr. Fishwell. I was hoping she was thinking about me.

I looked at the other kids. There are only fifteen, since its a lab. Not too many. And I noticed that the door to the hall is nice and large.

Anyway, that's when I got my first evil idea. Or maybe I should say, that's when my first evil idea got *me!*

Mr. Fishwell had just finished warning us about the dangers of playing with chemicals and was starting an experiment. With his chubby pink fingers, Mr. Fishwell poured chemicals from bottles into beakers, and from beakers into test tubes. Then he adjusted the gas jets for later on, when he'd be heating his mixture.

"Make sure you take notes," he announced. "You never know what's going to show up on the final. Now," continued Mr. Fishwell, "I'm going to pour the—"

That's when I leaped to my feet.

"Gas!" I shouted. "I smell gas!"

"Nonsense," said Mr. Fishwell, shaking his head so hard

all the flesh around his neck wiggled back and forth. "I just turned the gas off."

"But I do!" I insisted. "And I've got a sensitive nose. This room's gonna blow!"

Sondra started looking pale. Even Whip Wypikowski was getting nervous.

"Let's get outta here!" he said to one of his buddies.

"Stay in your seats! There is no gas leak!" stated Mr. Fishwell.

"C'mon, everybody!" I shouted, waving my arm toward the door. "Let's get out of here before it's too late!"

A race to the door followed. A few of the kids looked really scared. Most looked as though they just wanted to get away from Mr. Fishwell. I was glad no one tripped and got hurt. I don't want my evil twin to be *that* evil!

Soon the entire class was out in the hallway, pushing one another and having a good time. All except for Cindi Greenbottom, who was hyperventilating.

"Get back in this room!" bellowed Mr. Fishwell from the science lab.

"No way!" I said, shaking my head so hard my hair went flying despite all the mousse. "I'm not getting blown up just to watch some experiment!"

"Neither am I," said Sondra. "And my father's a lawyer, too!"

"Jellimiah Jensen," shouted Mr. Fishwell, "they should have kept you in reform school or wherever it was you were. And they should have locked the door and thrown away the key!"

"Reform school!" whistled Jake Cutter. He looked as though he was used to being the worst kid in school. "Whoa!"

"And his twin brother's such a goody-goody!" I heard

Sondra whisper to a girl named Valerie, who seems to be her best friend.

"You'll be back in reform school, too, young man, once Miss Thompson gets wind of this," threatened Mr. Fishwell. He'd joined us in the hallway. But seeing he was unable to shepherd us back into the lab, he ran off, probably looking for reinforcements.

"Should we stay so close to the lab?" worried Cindi. "What if it explodes right through the wall?"

"Aw, I wouldn't worry about that," I said soothingly.

Just then two sets of footsteps came echoing down the hallway. One was heavy, like an elephant's. That was Mr. Fishwell. The other was clip-clopping along on high heels. Something told me that was Miss Thompson.

I was right.

There she stood by the lab door. Her hand was on her hip and her nostrils were quivering violently.

"Young man!" she shrieked. "What is the meaning of this? Your brother would *never* act this way! Ruining Mr. Fishwell's class with some lie about gas! You should realize—"

But I never got to hear what it was I should realize.

The explosion was too loud.

Cindi Greenbottom was knocked right off her feet. Sondra ended up almost fainting into my arms. Whip looked like he might cry.

The explosion had come from the science lab. The glass in the door to the lab had been shattered. Luckily no one had been hit by the flying pieces.

I peered into the room.

What a mess!

The explosion had made a big black mark on the ceiling, and the whole place stank of gas. Practically every beaker, test tube, and bottle was broken. Puddles of chemicals were everywhere. I was just about to make a mean remark to Mr. Fishwell about playing with chemicals when a thought hit me. And it wasn't even an evil one.

"Hey!" I cried. "If it blew once, it could blow again!"

Little Cindi Greenbottom gave a tiny shriek and ran for her life. The rest of the class wasn't far behind, including Mr. Fishwell.

"We must evacuate the building in an organized manner and get the gas turned off," announced Miss Thompson. "And we must keep calm—very calm." But a second later she was charging down the hall on her giraffe legs, shouting, "Run for your lives! Run for your lives!"

Talk about keeping calm in an emergency!

Soon the entire building was evacuated onto the surrounding lawn and the gas had been shut off. The fire department came swooping down on Edgewood Junior High and inspected the damage.

"You were lucky," I heard the fire chief tell Miss Thompson. "If that classroom had had kids in it—well, I'd hate to think what might have happened."

"But there *was* a class in it," answered the hysterical Miss Thompson. "Luckily one of the students smelled gas and alerted the teacher, who, of course, led a calm and prudent evacuation from the room."

I was standing nearby and gave a smirk—a real one.

"We are always prepared at Edgewood Junior High," Miss Thompson told the fire chief. "I see to that."

"Well," said the fire chief, "my assistant tells me that one of the gas jets looks like it had a small leak. That would account for the smell and the explosion. Make sure you have the rest of them checked out before you turn the gas back on. And make sure you thank the kid who alerted the teacher."

"I shall, I shall," promised Miss Thompson.

But she never did.

She just glared at me as she sent us all to the cafeteria to start lunch early.

But I didn't care.

And I sure didn't eat lunch alone today!

It's almost dinnertime now and I'm sitting here in my room while Mom's downstairs cooking, but I still feel great.

There I was in the cafeteria, John Jensen—whoops, I mean Jellimiah!—the center of attention.

"Tell us how you did it!" cooed Sondra over her tuna fish sandwich.

"Next time you should leave old Fishface in the lab," suggested Jake Cutter.

"You've got quick reflexes," noted Whip. "No wonder you're such a star athlete!"

"And you've got such a sensitive nose!" cried Cindi.

I must have, I guess, though I never knew it until today.

But I suppose that without even knowing it, I smelled gas, and that's what gave me the idea to pretend I had.

Oh, well, even if Jellimiah wasn't as evil as I wanted him to be on his first day at school, at least he got to have lunch with Sondra Settle.

~

Friday, September 7, third period

"Carolyn Griffith." Mr. Sterling was taking attendance in homeroom earlier this morning.

"Here."

"Nanci Hester."

"Here."

"Jellimiah Jensen."

Silence.

"Jellimiah Jensen," repeated Mr. Sterling, looking up. I guess he was looking for Jellimiah's wild hair and ripped clothing. Instead he saw me. My hair was all neat and my clothes were pressed. "Where's your brother?" he wanted to know.

"Him?" I said, trying to sound as though I were hiding something. "He's . . . um . . ."

"Yes?" said Mr. Sterling, tapping a pen against his attendance book.

I hung my head in mock shame. "He had to see his parole officer," I mumbled. Come to think of it, I hope kids have parole officers. I should have checked before school, but I didn't think of it.

Mr. Sterling raised his eyebrows and shook his head. I hoped it was in disgust and not in disbelief. At least Jake Cutter seemed to believe it. He also seemed very impressed. So did Sondra Settle.

"John Jensen," continued Mr. Sterling, going down the roll. When he finished he looked up and said, "Jensen, we'll need a note from your parents explaining your absence yesterday, also your brother's today. If you don't have yours today, make sure I get both soon. Like Monday."

I wish it were Monday already. It's not that I like Mondays, it's just that I want to eat lunch again with Sondra. And I know she won't eat with John. It has to be Jellimiah. She won't even *talk* to me! But maybe she will.

Since Jellimiah was kind of a hit yesterday, I thought maybe I could be a hit, too. I decided in homeroom that would be my goal for today—to see if John could be as popular as Jellimiah. I didn't seem to be off to a good start, though—Sondra was completely ignoring me.

But then, just as we were heading off for first period, guess who came walking right over to me, obviously wanting to talk? Yes!

I was so excited I dropped my perfectly arranged loose-leaf notebook. Even as I sit here now in third-period study hall, I can feel it slipping out of my fingers.

"Ouch!" cried Sondra as my notebook fell like a bomb on her foot. "That hurt!"

"Sorry," I mumbled, and bent down to pick up my notebook. Of course the rings had opened and all the paper inside had come out. So there stood Sondra with a mountain of loose-leaf paper around her feet. And there I was, hoping no one would notice.

Of course they did. Jake smirked and Whip chuckled. Cindi Greenbottom looked worried. And a weird staring boy with a ponytail just stared all the harder.

"Yucky!" Sondra said, and kicked the papers I hadn't picked up yet away from where she was standing. There went my papers, flying all around the hallway. And there went my hope that John would ever impress Sondra.

I stood up, my notebook in my arms, all the paper I'd been able to cram back into it sticking out everywhere. I looked like someone who'd walked through a tornado.

"Is Jellimiah in a lot of trouble?" asked Sondra.

"A *lot,*" I said meaningfully. Out of the corner of my eye I saw last night's math homework, all neat and perfect. It lay across the hall where, instead of helping me pick it up, Sondra had kicked it. The next second it got trampled by some girl on her way to class. "A lot," I repeated, trying not to worry about my homework. I was hoping that if Sondra thought Jellimiah was *really* bad, maybe she'd lose interest in him and turn her attention to me, even if I had just dropped my notebook on her foot.

"Like what kind of trouble?" asked Sondra in a low voice.

I looked around me, as though I were making sure no one else was listening. "I'm not supposed to say," I told her as my math homework got kicked beneath the water fountain. "In fact, no one's allowed to talk about it, at least not until the trial."

"The trial!" gasped Sondra, her pretty eyes growing wider and wider. "That's neat!"

"Neat?" I began, but then Sondra rushed off to join her friend Valerie.

"Val!" she cried. "Jellimiah robbed a bank or something! He's going to have to stand trial!"

"Who told you?" Val wanted to know.

"Oh, his brother," replied Sondra. "That turkey just dropped his notebook right on my big toe. I may never cheerlead again!"

"What a dork," agreed Val, looking over at me trying to collect the rest of my papers from all around the hallway.

"*I* don't even think they're identical twins," announced Sondra, "no matter what anyone says. They don't even look alike," she added as she and Val passed out of earshot.

I was still pretending I hadn't heard the "turkey" part as I managed to gather all of my papers I could find. I noticed a few had been kicked into the girls' room. I hoped none of them were important.

I was racing along to math class, clutching my disheveled notebook, when I heard the late bell ring for first period. I ran faster. And faster. Maybe if I was just a minute late the teacher wouldn't mind. After all, I am new here. Not to mention the fact that Edgewood has a confusing rotating schedule, so every day is different.

Gasping for air, I stumbled into math class. Everyone was staring at me. They all had such weird looks on their faces, I quickly checked to see if my fly was down. (It wasn't.)

Then I saw Sondra. Wow! I figured she must have transferred into my math class, because she wasn't there yesterday or the day before. I wondered if she'd done it just to be near me. Or near Jellimiah, I should say.

"Sorry I'm late," I blurted out from the door, "but I . . . I dropped my notebook and I . . . I . . ."

"Sorry you're late?" said an annoyed voice from the blackboard. "I don't even know what you're doing here in the first place."

21

For the first time I noticed a black-haired woman holding a piece of chalk.

"Who—Who are you?" I asked. "And where's Mr. Trotter?"

"I am Señora Gonzales," she replied. "I imagine Señor Trotter is in his classroom, attempting to teach math. I am attempting to teach Spanish, if that's all right with you, young man."

The class laughed. Especially Sondra.

"Whoops!" I said. "I guess I'm in the wrong room," I added, backing out while the class kept on laughing. *Laugh all you like,* I was thinking. *Jellimiah will be back on Monday, and no one laughs at* him.

"So, Jensen," said Mr. Trotter as I stumbled into the correct classroom, "you decided to come to class after all."

"I dropped my notebook and then I got lost," I explained.

"I'll overlook it this time," replied Mr. Trotter. "Now sit down quietly and see if you can find last night's homework in that mare's nest of a notebook."

I sat down and rummaged through my notebook. Mr. Trotter kept on talking. I looked up at him for a moment. He's a youngish guy for a teacher, and a real jock. I'd learned he's the coach of the football team. He lives and breathes sports. Even the math problems he gives us involve sports. For example, if the Jets scored 20 percent more touchdowns this year than they did last year, and last year they scored 15 percent fewer than their all-time record, then how many touchdowns did they score this year? And he actually expects us to know what their all-time record is! Whip does, but I sure don't. I hate sports, mainly because I'm so bad at them. I think it goes back to fourth grade, when I went out for the baseball team. I was up at bat and I gave this mighty swing. Too bad I let go of the bat. And too bad it went flying off to the left—right through the windshield of the gym teacher's brand-new Mazda Miata. No wonder I got D's in gym from then on!

At last I found my math homework.

I got up and haded it to Mr. Trotter.

Mr. Trotter looked at the homework and then at me.

"John," he said in that cat-and-mouse way teachers have, "can I ask you something?"

I nodded. I noticed the rest of the class leaning forward to listen.

"Do you always think it's necessary to *wash* your homework before you hand it in?" asked Mr. Trotter.

"What do you mean, wash it?" I asked with a sinking feeling in my chest.

Mr. Trotter held up my homework for all the class to see.

The top third was fine. But the bottom two thirds were a mess. There were all these shoe prints everywhere. And the paper was all damp, and the ink was runny and impossible to read. I was in such a hurry to hand it in I hadn't noticed.

"It was under the drinking fountain—" I started to explain.

"Next time," said Mr. Trotter, "I suggest you keep your homework in a drier place."

I hung my head as the class laughed. I was wishing I were Jellimiah today. *He* would have figured out something smart to do. Well, at least Sondra isn't in this math class. But Whip is, and he'll probably tell Sondra. I think they're friends.

"One more thing, Jensen," said Mr. Trotter. "Where's your brother?"

"He'll be back Monday," I said.

"Good," said Mr. Trotter.

Good? I thought. Since when would a straight arrow like Mr. Trotter be happy to see a no-good kid like Jellimiah? *I'm* the one he should be happy to see! I mean, Mr. Trotter and I even kind of dress alike: our shirts are always ironed and our pants are always pressed.

"Yes," continued Mr. Trotter, "I've heard he's one heck of a quarterback. I wanted to see when his leg would be healed enough to try out for the Panthers. I don't suppose you play, too?" he asked, looking at me almost as if I were an insect.

"Not really," I said.

"It must be somewhat rare, statistically speaking, for one identical twin to be a star athlete and the other to be, well . . ."

Mr. Trotter didn't finish the sentence. He didn't have to.

The entire class seemed to be looking at me in disgust. Except for the kid with the ponytail. I'd learned his name was Albert Causley. But he was probably daydreaming anyway.

Before I knew it, math class was ending and Mr. Trotter was announcing a quiz for Monday. But that doesn't apply to *me!* On Monday Jellimiah will be back. I'll make him flunk that quiz. Then we'll see how long Mr. Trotter thinks my evil twin is so great.

I was on my way here, to study hall, when I heard my name being called over the school's intercom: "John Jensen to Miss Thompson's office; John Jensen to Miss Thompson's office."

Jake Cutter snickered as I passed him in the hall. He knew where I was going. He probably thinks I *like* going there!

Miss Thompson was sitting at her desk. She didn't look too happy.

"John," she said, clutching a piece of paper in her long fingers, "this just came."

My heart sank. Had she found out I'd been lying? Leave it to nosy Miss Thompson to track down my real records in all of California! How on earth was I going to get out of this one?

"It's for Jellimiah," she said in a tense voice.

"What?" I said. How could someone who doesn't exist be receiving mail?

"It's from the Edgewood Fire Department," she explained. "It just arrived. It's . . . it's . . . well, it's a citation for bravery for getting the class out of the science lab before the gas explosion."

Miss Thompson handed me the citation. "Make sure your brother gets it," she said.

"Consider it already given to him," I said.

"Thank you, John," said Miss Thompson. "You're such a dear—"

But just then Miss Thompson's secretary buzzed her. Miss Thompson picked up her phone. "Yes, Ms. Betterton?" I heard her say. "Who's on the line? . . . Yes, I'll take it. It's an important call," she added to me, nodding me toward the door.

I've been sitting here for the last ten minutes looking at that citation. They'll probably put Jellimiah on one of those real-life TV shows. Maybe they'll even re-create the event: "Teen Saves Science Class!" Jellimiah will be famous. And I'll still be his turkey twin brother! I mean, if they put him on TV, it's not as though I can go along and be introduced to America, too.

I can't help it. I'm jealous. Jealous of myself.

Friday, September 7, after school

Lunch. Alone. That's the John Jensen story.

There I sat, right in the middle of the cafeteria, like a black hole in the middle of the universe.

". . . I can't wait until the party!" I heard Sondra telling Val two tables to my left. It might as well have been two miles. "I'm inviting Jellimiah," she added.

"I hear that new kid is a major athlete," Whip was saying to some of his football buddies.

". . . and he was even in reform school!" Jake was boasting to some very impressed-looking kids.

"I know he saved my life!" Cindi gasped to a girl with braces.

They were all talking about Jellimiah! No one was talking about me! No one was even talking *to* me!

Well, at least I was hungry and I'd brought some great soup in my thermos.

I was about to pull it out of my backpack when I happened to look around me.

Sondra and Val were eating french fries, Whip was downing meat loaf, and Jake was demolishing a piece of pepperoni pizza.

No one had brought food from home. No one.

Except for me.

I noticed Sondra observing me from the corner of her eye. I couldn't let her—or anyone else—see me eating food from home! I'll never get popular *that* way!

My stomach was rumbling, but I didn't pull out my thermos.

I just sat there.

I hadn't brought any money, so I couldn't go and buy food like the other kids.

I just kept on sitting there.

All alone. And starved, too. I hoped no one could hear my rumbling stomach.

I was the only kid sitting alone—except for Albert Causley. But he looked as though he didn't mind. He was busy drawing in a sketchpad.

With my stomach still rumbling, I made my way to English class. I was in honors English. The teacher, Mr. Forester, is the most popular teacher at Edgewood. He doesn't even make us sit in assigned seats. That meant I had to figure out where I should sit.

I looked around the classroom to see if anyone looked as though they wanted me to sit next to them.

No one did.

Then I looked to see if there was anyone who looked as though they wouldn't mind if I sat next to them.

The only person like that was Cindi Greenbottom, but there weren't any seats empty near her.

I hate being the new kid. But then, I wasn't much more popular back in Los Angeles when I was an "old" kid.

I decided I'd just sit alone in the back of the room.

I was heading down the aisle when I saw her. She sat in the third row. She had thick, curly brown hair and bright brown eyes. Her skin was pale. She was wearing this blouse with embroidery all over it. And she looked serious. Smart, too. I wondered who she was. She seemed to be smiling shyly in my direction.

I got nearer and nearer to where she was sitting. There was even an empty seat next to hers! Should I sit there? Was she smiling at me? What should I do?

I slowed down as I got near her, trying to figure out if she was really smiling at me. But when I was about three steps away, she glanced down at her desk. I figured if she'd wanted me to sit near her, she wouldn't have looked away. But she did.

I kept on going.

But just as I walked by her, she looked up again. And it seemed as though she was looking for me! But by then I had passed her desk and the empty seat. I couldn't double back. I couldn't be that obvious. That's the kind of thing Jellimiah can do, not John. And besides, I thought, what if she wasn't smiling at me, but at someone walking behind me?

I decided I should sit down next to her anyway. I turned around casually—and bumped into a blond boy with glasses as he sat down next to her. I was so surprised I almost dropped my notebook again.

I went and sat at the back of the room. All alone. Like I was in quarantine or something.

I noticed the curly-haired girl chatting happily with the blond boy.

She was probably smiling at him all along.

My thoughts were soon distracted by Mr. Forester. Toward the end of class he told us that as an honors class, we'll be writing and printing our own literary magazine. He pointed out some boxes in the back of the room.

"That's our new desktop publishing system," he said. "The computers just came today."

That gave me an idea. Somehow I'll write something so outstanding for the literary magazine that everybody in the class will admire me. And I'll write something so pathetic as Jellimiah (he's in honors English, too) that everybody will hate him.

And maybe I can even find a way to do something to help Mr. Forester. If I help the most popular teacher, then perhaps some popularity will rub off on me. Maybe Mr. Forester will fall in the pond near school and I can rescue him from drowning. No, wait—that won't work. I'm a terrible swimmer, even if I am from California.

In the meantime, though, I wanted to find some way to show off in class. I got an opportunity a few minutes into the class, when Mr. Forester said, "Now, does anyone have any suggestions for our magazine?"

My class in Los Angeles also had its own magazine. It was even pretty good. I decided I could tell them all about that. I could even claim I'd been the editor! The kids here would never know I'd written just one story for it and that only the second half of the story was printed, because the first half got lost—and no one even noticed it started in the middle.

I raised my hand and was soon called on.

"My class in Los Angeles had a literary magazine," I began in a quiet voice.

"Can you speak louder?" asked the blond boy. "I can hardly hear you."

"I can't, either," agreed Cindi, cupping her hand around her ear.

"John," said Mr. Forester, "how about coming to the front of the room and telling us all about it?"

"Okay, I guess," I said, and got up.

I hate speaking in front of big groups! I can never remember what I want to say. I do all right if I'm sitting down. And if I have notes. Maybe that's why I took my notebook with me.

"I'm . . . I'm from Los Angeles," I began, "and we . . . we . . . we . . ."

The class looked at me. I looked at them. And looked. My mind had gone completely blank. I couldn't think of a thing. Not one thing.

"Go on," said Mr. Forester gently,.

"Um . . . we . . . um . . ." I mumbled. "I mean, um . . . well . . ."

I looked down at my loose-leaf binder for inspiration. Nothing came to me. Then my elbow started to itch. I went to scratch it, but it was hard to do with my notebook in my hand. I transferred the notebook to under my other arm. I was hoping that once I got rid of the itch I'd be able to think clearly.

"It was, well . . . sort of like . . ." I began, scratching and trying to think at the same time.

The blond boy was staring at me as though I were a lunatic. The curly-haired girl was looking embarrassed. Cindi was leaning forward expectantly. Albert seemed fascinated.

"How often did you publish issues?" asked Mr. Forester.

I turned to answer him.

"Three," I said, meaning three times a year.

"What did he say?" asked the blond boy.

I turned back to tell him what I meant.

I guess I turned too fast.

"Whoops!" I cried as my left foot went sliding to the left on the newly waxed floor and my right foot suddenly slipped backward. I thought for sure I was going to fall on my rear end in front of the entire class. But luckily I *am* kind of coordinated. At the last second I flailed my arms and regained my balance.

I shoved my hands casually into my pants pockets, trying not to blush too much. Then suddenly I remembered my notebook. Where was it? I looked on the floor, but it wasn't there. I twisted around and looked behind me, but it wasn't there, either.

"Hey, Jensen!"

I turned back around and saw the blond boy waving my notebook in the air. I must have thrown it when I was flailing my arms. I guess he caught it on the fly.

He handed it back to me as the class dissolved into laughter.

I blushed bright red and slunk back to my seat.

Mr. Forester quieted the class and reminded them that I was new and maybe shy in front of so many strange faces.

I blushed all the more, since I'd blown my big chance to impress the class and Mr. Forester.

At last the period was over and I could get out of there. I'm not sure, but I think that as we were leaving the room the curly-haired girl smiled at me. Probably she just feels sorry for me. At any rate, when I saw her looking at me, I blushed again.

I think I was still blushing at three o'clock when I was

heading home. I was hurrying down the hall. I wanted to get out of there.

But I'd forgotten my math book, so I had to hurry back to my locker.

I was so busy hurrying that I practically bumped into a custodian who was fumbling with his key in front of Mr. Forester's classroom.

"If you're looking for Mr. Forester," I said, "he told us he was leaving right after class. And that was fifth period."

"Uh, do you think he's coming back today?" asked the custodian.

"I don't think so," I said. "But I'm not sure about his schedule. I'm new here."

"I see," said the custodian, fitting his key into the lock. "That's okay. I'm just doing a favor for Mr. Forester. He doesn't have to be here."

"A favor?" I said. "Can I help?"

"Well," said the custodian, "I *could* use some help. It's these computers. We just found out they're defective. They've got to go back to the supplier and be replaced. It's a good thing they're still under warranty."

"That's for sure," I agreed. I got busy helping the custodian cart the computers down the hall to where a friend of his had backed a van up to the school. It only took around twenty minutes and was a lot easier than rescuing Mr. Forester from drowning. I'm a good worker. Besides, we had an easy time of it—there was some kind of big game one town over, so Edgewood had emptied out quickly. Only geeks like me, with pressed pants and neatly combed hair, hang around school when there's something better to do. Besides, no one had invited me to go with them. The only person I saw while we were moving the computers was that curly-haired girl from English class, but since I'm sure she likes that blond boy more than me, I ignored her.

"Thanks for your help!" said the custodian, getting into the van, which his friend drove off quickly.

"Anytime!" I called after him, feeling good about myself. I know it's not much, but at least I did something to make up for acting like such a fool in English class.

I don't think I can take another weekend like this past one: no friends, no dates, no phone calls, no nothing. John Jensen sure hasn't made a big impression at Edgewood Junior High! And Jellimiah was there only one day last week.

Well, this is the week that is going to change things.

I figured out a few things over the weekend as I hung out with Mom.

First, I realized that I can keep up this twin business only through Friday. I mean, at some point someone has to start wondering why Jellimiah and John Jensen are never seen at the same time in the same place.

Second, I also realized that I can use Jellimiah to make people start liking me (John) a little, or at least start noticing me. People listen to Jellimiah when he says something. So why shouldn't he start saying good things about me? The only problem is that I know as little about inventing things to make me popular as I do about devising things to make Jellimiah seem evil.

Third, I've decided to have as much fun with Jellimiah as I can. Why have an evil twin if you don't make him as evil as possible?

I was walking down the hallway this morning thinking about all this, my blond hair all moussed and wild and my clothes all ripped and ragged. Since I'm Jellimiah again today, I'm also wearing my too-big black boots that flop around when I walk and make a nice thumping noise. You can tell Jellimiah Jensen is coming a mile away, and that's just how I want it. Suddenly I heard a *thump, thump, thump* from behind me. At first I thought it was some weird kind of echo. Then I looked around and saw Jake Cutter.

He looked just like me! His hair was all moussed up like crazy. His clothes were all ripped. And he was wearing boots that were a few sizes too big!

"Hey, man," he said as he thumped past.

"Hey," I called after him.

At least Jellimiah's made some kind of impression!

Mr. Sterling was still not impressed, though.

"What do you and John do," he demanded, "take turns coming to school?"

I gave one of my Jellimiah smirks.

"Nah, man," I said, "it's not like that." I was about to say that never being at school on the same day with a jerk like John would be a good idea, when I remembered that from now on I'm going to praise John whenever possible. Especially when Sondra Settle is around.

"Then where is your brother?" persisted Mr. Sterling.

"It's like this," I said, putting my praise-John plan into action. "John's absent 'cause he, um, wrote this great story last year," I told Mr. Sterling, "and it was so great he got the

Pomona Prize. And they're, um, calling him on the phone to interview him about how great he is, 'cause he's also a great surfer. In fact, he won the Malibu Master Competition. Anyway, he had to stay home and be there for the phone call."

"Interesting," said Mr. Sterling, but I couldn't help noticing that none of the kids in homeroom seemed especially interested. Sondra was fiddling with her fingernails and Albert looked more amused than impressed. "I'm glad at least one of you twins is a productive citizen," continued Mr. Sterling. "And speaking of being productive, can you produce written excuses for your absences? You should have brought them in by now."

"Yeah," I said, "my mom wrote 'em. But I guess I lost 'em."

"Well, find them," said Mr. Sterling sternly. "Don't let *your* carelessness get your brother in trouble."

"I'll think about it," I said.

"How's your ligament?" asked Whip when Mr. Sterling had finished taking attendance.

"My what?"

"Your ligament. The thing in your leg you hurt waterskiing," said Whip.

"Oh, that," I said. "It's still broken."

"Broken?" said Whip. "I thought you said it was twisted."

"Twisted, broken—what's the difference? It still hurts. Why do you want to know?"

" 'Cause football tryouts are coming up, and we need to know ahead of time who's going out for the team," explained Whip.

"I'm not sure I'll be better by next week," I said, acting sad about it.

"What about the week after?" demanded Whip. "We don't start practice until then."

"Yeah," I said, "I should be better by then." I'll also be gone. Jellimiah will be history, having passed his mantle of popularity to his marvelous twin brother, John.

"Great," said Whip. "We could really use a top-rated quarterback. And that's you, since your brother Jim's such a wimp!"

Whip didn't even know my name! That's when I decided to get a little evil with Whip.

"We'll see," I said nonchalantly.

"What do you mean, we'll see?" demanded Whip.

"I meant just what I said," I answered. "Maybe I will, maybe I won't. I've got other things to do besides go out for the football team."

"But we really need a good quarterback," repeated Whip. "And there should be room on the team for—"

"Whip!" barked Mr. Sterling. "Don't let Jellimiah be a bad influence on you! Homeroom is for silent preparation, not idle chatter."

"Yes, sir," said Whip, looking down at his desk. I gave an exaggerated yawn to show Mr. Sterling what I thought about him and his rules. Why shouldn't we talk if we want to? We're not in prison, we're in junior high school!

"Hi, Jellimiah, I'm glad you're back in school," cooed Sondra as we made our way out of homeroom to our first-period classes. "You're way cool, and your brother's, like, *such* a dweeb. Who cares if he won some dumb old prize?"

"It's a really important prize," I said. "Really."

Sondra gave a sweet smile. "You're so cute when you stand up for your jerk of a brother," she said. "If he were *my* brother, when I moved I would have left him behind."

"You've got him all wrong," I told Sondra. "He's a good surfer, too."

"Yucky!" said Sondra. "Surfing's so . . . so *California!* No one at Edgewood would be caught *dead* surfing. I'm glad *you* don't surf or anything like that."

I was in the middle of praying Whip wouldn't repeat the story I'd told him about Jellimiah being a triple-class-rated water-skier when Sondra's best friend, Val, came panting over.

"Have you heard?" she cried excitedly. "It's all over school!"

"What's all over school?" asked Sondra. "Tell me!"

"Well," began Val, "I heard Janine telling—"

"Girls!" interrupted the stern voice of Mr. Trotter. "Do you plan to stand chatting in the hall, or can we expect you in math class sometime this century?"

"Sorry, Mr. Trotter," said Sondra. "We were just saying how much we enjoyed last night's homework."

Sondra and Val went into math class and I headed off for my Monday first-period class, English.

The mood in English class was weird. *Really* weird.

Mr. Forester was standing kind of slumped in the front of the room. He had a pained expression on his face.

I made my way to an empty seat next to the girl with curly hair and brown eyes, beating out the blond boy with glasses by three seconds.

She gave me a half smile.

"Hey there," I said. "My friends call me Jellimiah."

"I already know your name," she said. "It's a small school."

"I don't know yours yet," I said, running my hand through my moussed hair and thumping my boots on the classroom floor.

"It's Missy," she said, "and I don't feel like talking. I'm too upset."

"About what?" I asked, but just at that moment the classroom door opened and in stalked Miss Thompson.

Miss Thompson joined Mr. Forester at the front of the room. Her nostrils were quivering violently and a vein in her neck was throbbing. Those are not good signs. Mr. Forester just looked sad.

"Class," began Miss Thompson, addressing the group but staring at me, "something has occurred. Something dreadful."

I noticed Missy squirming uncomfortably. She even shot me a pitying look. I didn't have any idea what that was about.

Miss Thompson pressed her long fingers together, then started to speak.

"There has been a burglary," she announced. Some of the class gasped. Many, like Missy, seemed already to know all about it. I realized that this was what Val had been trying to tell Sondra about.

"What did they take?" asked the blond boy from the back of the room.

"Well, Nicholas," said Miss Thompson, getting her worried-giraffe look, "I regret to tell you that someone somehow managed to break into your classroom and steal each and every one of our new computers."

A gasp rose from the room.

"But how?" cried Cindi, peering around nervously. She looked as though she was scared the burglar was still lurking somewhere in the classroom.

"This we do not yet know," replied Miss Thompson, still staring at me. "But we aim to find out. And find out we shall," she added in a threatening voice, staring all the harder at me. "We shall have to ascertain the whereabouts of, um, certain students last Friday afternoon. Jellimiah Jensen—were *you* near this classroom at any time last Friday?"

"Jellimiah was absent Friday," Mr. Forester told her.

"Oh, dear," said Miss Thompson in a disappointed voice. "I'd forgotten about that."

Looking back on it now, it's clear I was pretty slow on the uptake. But it was only then that I figured it out. For a second I thought my heart would stop beating.

What a jerk I was!

That was no custodian last Friday. And those computers weren't defective. They were still in their boxes. They hadn't even been used once. Even if they were defective, no one would have known it yet. And they weren't going back to any supplier. They were being stolen. No wonder the driver sped off before I could a good look at his face. And I helped! Me—John!

If only it had been Jellimiah!

But it was me. The real me.

I didn't do it on purpose, though. It wasn't my fault.

Feeling awful, I sneaked a glance around the classroom. I was glad no one knew I was involved.

And then it hit me. Missy! She'd been there on Friday; she'd seen me (John) helping to load the computer into the van.

No wonder Missy had given me (Jellimiah) that look! She felt sorry for me because she thought my brother was a thief! I was hoping against hope that she wouldn't tell.

Now Mr. Forester was speaking.

". . . if any of you has any idea about who took our computers, please, *please* tell either Miss Thompson or me—right now, or in private, if you prefer."

Miss Thompson was looking even more anguished. Her

vein was bulging like one of those fat ropes they make you climb in gym class as if you were Tarzan or something.

"I hate to be the one to tell you this," she said, her nostrils all aquiver, "but this is the third burglary here at Edgewood since school opened."

Cindi let loose with a tiny shriek and looked ready to run for her life.

"Also there's been some vandalism," continued Miss Thompson, "perhaps even including tampering with the gas jets in Mr. Fishwell's science lab. Other schools in the area have experienced similar problems, I understand. We were hoping to avoid them with the new night watchman we just hired, but, well, that hasn't been so. If these burglaries persist, we shall have to hire more guards and install more antitheft devices. And that would cost us a great deal of money. In fact, we might have to drop certain courses to pay for it—like honors English."

Silence fell over the room, broken only by the sound of Cindi starting to hyperventilate.

Everyone looked unhappy. Especially Missy. I could tell she was trying to make up her mind about something. I just hoped it wasn't what I thought it was.

I closed my eyes and prayed she'd keep her mouth shut until I could tell her what really happened.

"Yes, Missy?" said Miss Thompson in her crisp voice.

"Um," said Missy nervously, twisting her curly hair around a finger, "I, um, think I might have seen something."

"Please go on," said Miss Thompson.

Missy looked down at her desk and blushed. She seemed to be avoiding looking in my direction.

"It was just after school Friday," she began, "and I was getting some stuff from my locker. And I saw a man loading computer boxes into a van. I didn't think anything about it at the time. I just figured he was taking away the empty boxes."

"I see," said Miss Thompson. "Would you recognize this man if you saw him again? And was he working alone?"

Missy blushed again. "I'm not sure I'd recognize him. I mostly saw his back, you see, so it might be hard. In fact, I think I probably couldn't recognize him."

"Was he working alone?" repeated Miss Thompson.

"I think I saw someone else in the van," said Missy nervously. "And . . . and . . ."

"And what?" demanded Miss Thompson.

"I'm not sure," mumbled Missy, staring down at her desk.

"Not sure of what?" Miss Thompson wanted to know.

"I'm not sure . . . not sure how many, um, people were helping him."

"How can you not be sure?" cried Miss Thompson. "You know how to count!"

"Perhaps it's something Missy would feel more comfortable telling us in private," suggested Mr. Forester.

Missy looked up with a relieved expression. I felt kind of relieved, too. "Yes," she said, brushing her hair back. "I'd .. I'd rather talk to you alone. Maybe there's some reason or something . . . I . . . I . . ."

"That's all right, Missy," said Mr. Forester. "We can go out into the hall and speak privately."

"That's good," said Missy. "I'd hate to tell on someone if I was wrong, especially a new kid like John Jensen."

As soon as the words were out of her mouth Missy looked horrified. I thought she was going to cry. I thought *I* was going to cry.

"I didn't mean to say his name!" Missy burst out. "I didn't!"

"John Jensen!" exclaimed Miss Thompson in a loud voice,

just in case a few of the kids in the class hadn't heard. "You saw John Jensen assisting the burglar? I simply do not believe it! Are you quite sure, young woman?"

"Yes," said Missy in a strangled voice. She was still staring down at her desk. I felt sorry for her. She hadn't meant to tell in front of everyone, I knew that.

"Jellimiah," barked out Miss Thompson, "do you happen to know anything about this?"

"Um," I began, "well . . . I, um, well . . ."

"I can't hear him," complained Nick.

"Perhaps Jellimiah would prefer to talk to us in private," suggested Mr. Forester.

"Nonsense," disagreed Miss Thompson. "We shall have it out here and now. Stand up so we can hear you," she ordered.

I stood up.

Help! I thought. I was going to have to speak to the entire class again. And without notes! I remembered what had happened the last time. If I froze up again, everyone would think John was a burglar. It wasn't fair. John was supposed to be the good twin!

"Please begin," said Miss Thompson in a cold voice.

"Well, um," I said, "it's like—"

"Stop stalling," hissed Miss Thompson.

"And speak up," put in Nick.

I knew the more I hemmed and hawed, the worse it would look. I had to think quickly.

"My brother's no thief," I said loudly, at last finding my Jellimiah voice. "No way, nohow. He even won an award from the police chief in Los Angeles for being the most honest kid in town. It''s called the, um, the George Washington Junior Award. And he won it. Twice, in fact. Yeah, twice."

"That's very nice," said Mr. Forester, "but we're talking about what happened on Friday."

"Oh, that," I said. "Friday. Well," I continued, "well . . ." I glanced at the faces around me. Everyone was looking at me—staring, even. Nick and Missy, Albert and Cindi—everyone. It was like my worst nightmare. I took a deep breath. *You're Jellimiah,* I said to myself. *You can do it. You can do it!*

I stared back at the class and began.

"John was just leaving school," I said, "and he walked right into this man wearing a custodian's uniform. How was he supposed to know he didn't work here? We've only gone to this school for four days. He never dreamed he was a burglar because he had a key to the room."

"He had a key?" shrieked Miss Thompson. "But that's impossible!"

"No, it isn't," I said in a voice that no one could doubt—my Jellimiah voice. "This man was dressed like a custodian and he had a key. He told John he was taking defective computers back to the supplier, and John offered to help. He's very helpful, among the many other good qualities that have won him so many awards, including the—"

"Skip it with the awards," grumbled Nick. "Who cares about awards, anyway?"

"Yeah," I said, stalling again. I hadn't realized *nobody* cared about all those awards I'd been making up.

"Are you done?" asked Miss Thompson.

"Not quite," I said. "I just want to say that John had absolutely no idea that he was assisting in burglary. None whatsoever," I added forcefully. "I've known John all my life. In fact, I almost know him better than I know myself, and I'm telling you he would never ever in a million years do anything like this on purpose. No," I concluded in a loud, clear voice, "my brother, John, is guilty only of making a mistake, not of being a thief. No one is more honest than he is. No one. John Jensen is one great kid."

To my astonishment, the class burst into loud applause when I finished—even Miss Thompson!

"So it *was* a mistake," said Mr. Forester. "Well, at least there's a chance John could provide us with a description of the burglar. Do you think he'd be able to recognize him?"

"Maybe," I said. "But John was so busy helping, he didn't get that good a look at the man's face. And he didn't see the face of the man in the van at all."

"Gosh," said Albert, a strange smile on his face, "how do you know so much about it? You sound like you were there."

"John and I are very close," I replied. "Almost like one person. We're absolutely identical twins, so we share all our secrets. John told me everything about what happened at school on Friday when I was absent."

And having said that, I sat down in my seat.

Yes! I had done it! They all believed me. I mean, why shouldn't they? I was telling the truth. But I know that John could never have convinced them. Never.

My thoughts were interrupted by a weird whooshing sound.

It was coming from Cindi Greenbottom. She was starting to hyperventilate big time.

"But what if the burglar comes back?" Cindi was gasping. "I've got sixteen dollars and twenty-eight cents in my purse! He might steal it when I'm not looking!"

"Calm down, Cindi," said Mr. Forester gently. "I'm sure our burglar is far away by now—if he has any sense, that is."

∾

Monday, September 10, after school

I had a crowd around me at lunch today. There was Sondra, cooing at me dreamily. Val and Whip were there. Even Cindi, who'd finally stopped hyperventilating.

"Hey, tell us about your drippy brother," said Val. "I can't believe he was such a jerk. Gosh, how many computers did he help steal?"

"Maybe he'll have to stand trial, too," said Sondra.

I really wish I hadn't made up that bit about Jellimiah standing trial. It could make John look bad. People might think being a criminal runs in our family.

"John didn't steal those computers," I said in my impressive Jellimiah voice. "And he made up that bit about the trial," I went on. "He's got a good imagination. That's why he won the Pomona Prize," I added from force of habit.

"You mean you don't have to stand trial?" asked Sondra, all disappointed.

Good grief—I'd gotten John off the hook, but now Son-dra would think Jellimiah was a bore. That wasn't what I had in mind.

"Nah," I said in an offhand way. "I don't have to stand trial." Then, in a low voice, I added darkly, "I'm too smart to get caught."

"Ooh!" said Sondra. "I like that!"

"Speaking of getting caught, when will they catch the burglar who stole those computers? I'm so nervous I don't know what to do," Cindi was saying. But I wasn't paying attention to her—I'd just noticed Missy Einhorn sitting only a table away. I couldn't help thinking that maybe she'd sat there just to be near me.

". . . wait till I tell my father," Sondra was now saying. "If anything happens to me or anything I own, he'll sue the skirt off Miss Thompson. He's a lawyer, you know," she added. "In fact, he's the . . ."

My attention went back to Missy. She was eating a yogurt and looked like she was waiting for something. Or someone.

Maybe she was waiting for me!

I was just about to get up and saunter past her table in my thumpy boots when I saw what she was waiting for— I mean, *who* she was waiting for.

Up came that blond guy with glasses. Nick. I'd learned his last name was Clarke.

What a fool I was to think she'd been waiting for *me,* even if I was Jellimiah Jensen, not John.

I turned around in time to hear Sondra finish her sentence.

". . . and that's how much money he makes, and I'm not lying."

"Cool," said Whip, munching his third sandwich.

Just then I felt a tap on my shoulder.

"May I talk with you a second?" asked a pretty voice.

I looked up. I dropped my sandwich and almost spilled my milk. For a second I nearly forgot I was Jellimiah.

"Yes," I said. Then, quickly, I said, "I mean, yeah. What's up?"

"It's kind of private," said Missy.

"Yeah, all right," I said in my Jellimiah voice. "We can step outside for a minute."

As Missy and I made our way to the terrace next to the cafeteria, I could hear Sondra saying to Val, "She is *so* gross! I'm not going to invite *her* to—"

But then the door slammed shut and Missy and I were alone. Even now, writing alone in my room at home, I can remember the moment like it's happening right this second.

She isn't exactly pretty, but there's just something about her. She looks like she knows who she is, if you know what I mean. I felt pleased because she'd left that Nick kid just to talk to me. Maybe she was going to drop him, I started thinking. Maybe she had a thing for blond guys. Maybe she was about to ask me for a date.

"Jellimiah," she said, "can you do me a favor?"

"Maybe," I said, giving a shrug but not feeling so cool inside.

"Can you tell John that I'm sorry I told on him, even if it was by mistake? I should have known someone as neat as he is wouldn't have done something like that on purpose."

"Neat?" I said in disbelief.

"Yes," continued Missy, "it felt weird telling on someone I like."

"You like him?" I gasped.

Missy blushed a bit but didn't answer the question.

"I've got to go," she said. "Nick is waiting for me."

48

She left me alone on the terrace, shaking my moussed head.

What a day! The boring twin gets accused of stealing computers and the interesting twin doesn't interest the girl—*she* likes the boring one! Oh, well, it isn't all bad, I guess. At least I know Missy likes John, even if it is only as a friend. I mean, she already has a boyfriend, that blond guy, Nick.

I was just heading back in when I heard a horrible sound: *Clip-clop, clip-clop.* Only one person clip-clops like that.

I turned around.

I was right.

There she stood.

"Jellimiah," said Miss Thompson in a frosty voice, "I've been looking for you."

"Well, congratulations, you found me," I replied, trying to look blasé.

"I've got my eye on you," continued Miss Thompson.

"Enjoy the view," I replied.

Her nostrils vibrated when she heard that remark, but she kept right on talking. "I've got my suspicions, young man. I am almost ready to believe that it was you, disguised as your dear brother, who assisted in Friday's burglary, except—well, except you two are so different, even though you are twins, that I think it would be impossible for one of you to imitate the other. Impossible!"

"I wouldn't imitate that dork if you paid me," I said. I can still say mean things about John to Miss Thompson. I don't care what *she* thinks of him!

"And where is your dear brother?" asked Miss Thompson.

I gave a Jellimiah shrug, then a Jellimiah smirk. "He kinda hurt his wrist again."

Miss Thompson shuddered. "One day," she said, "you

shall realize the error of your ways. I just hope you won't be in jail at the time!"

"Aw, go lock yourself up and leave me alone!" I muttered.

"Watch your manners, young man!" said Miss Thompson. "And watch your step!"

Then she stepped away, *clip-clop, clip-clop,* and I stepped back into the cafeteria just in time for lunch to be over and math to be starting.

That meant it was make-Mr.-Trotter-hate-Jellimiah time. I got ready to have some fun.

"Take your seats and get ready for our first quiz," announced Mr. Trotter as we entered. "Make sure your pencils are sharpened. And make sure you keep quiet. This *is* a quiz."

"Quizzes are so stupid," I said. "Especially *math* quizzes."

"Let's settle down, please," said Mr. Trotter.

"Jellimiah's way right," began Jake. "Quizzes are—"

"Quiet, Jake!" ordered Mr. Trotter, handing out the quizzes.

"Multiple choice," I sneered. "I *hate* multiple choice."

"Yes," agreed Mr. Trotter, "multiple-choice quizzes *are* less challenging. I don't care for them myself. But it's how they do the questions on college admissions tests, and we have to bear that in mind."

"But it's not fair, man!" I shouted. "I didn't know there was going to be a quiz today!"

For a second Mr. Trotter's expression changed, and I was sure I'd finally gotten to him. Then his expression changed back and he said, "If you're half as good at math as you are at football, I'm sure you'll do just fine."

Soon all the quizzes had been given out and the class got to work. I looked at the first question and knew right away the answer was B. (I can't help it if I've always been good at math.) I peeked to my left and saw Whip struggling with his calculations. He looked over at me looking at him, grunted, and filled in the answer to question one. D, he wrote. And that's probably the grade he's going to get. Poor Whip. You have to have at least a C average to stay on the football team.

Jake was absentmindedly kicking his floppy boot against the leg of his desk. The leg was loose, so each time he kicked it, it made a little grating noise. *Thunk, screech! Thunk, screech!*

"Jake Cutter!" barked Mr. Trotter. "If you can't keep quiet, I'll take your quiz from you this very instant and write a big F on top."

Jake did his best to give a Jellimiah-style smirk but kept his foot still from then on.

Hmm, I thought. *So noise annoys Trotter. That's an easy one.*

I began whistling softly.

I whistle as well as I play football and as well as I surf. In other words, I'm about the world's worst whistler.

Mr. Trotter looked up in exasperation.

"Who the heck is—" he began. Then he stopped. He'd figured out who the heck it was. "That's nice whistling there, Jellimiah," he said. "But please save it for after class."

I couldn't believe it. Nothing seemed to annoy this guy. At least, nothing *I* did.

Well, at least I knew one thing Trotter wouldn't like. I proceeded to totally blow his dumb quiz. I didn't even read the questions. I just whizzed through it picking answers at random till I got to the end. I won't just get an F—I'll probably get a zero! Boy, am I going to have fun flunking things as Jellimiah! I've always wanted to write really stupid answers to those dumb tests teachers are always giving us. They wouldn't like it if we made *them* take tests all the time.

"Math is go gross," I said in a loud voice.

"Oh, Jellimiah," said Mr. Trotter, "you're such a jokester! Just make sure you're serious about taking care of that ligament of yours. The Panthers need you!"

I saw Sondra in the hall on the way to study hall. She gave me the sweetest smile and I forgot all about Missy. I had to make Sondra change her mind about John. I had to.

"Hey there, Sondra," I said in my cool Jellimiah voice.

"Hi, Jellimiah," cooed Sondra. "I wish we could talk, but if I'm late again for history, Mr. Morris will give me detention or something. He's so mean to me, it just isn't fair."

"John and I will take care of him if he hassles you," I said, giving a smirk.

"I know you would do *anything* to *anybody,*" agreed Sondra. "But your brother?"

"John's cooler than he lets on," I told her.

"Really?" said Sondra. "Maybe. But no one's as cool as you, not even Jake."

And with that she hurried off to history.

All right! I told myself as I headed for study hall. For once Sondra didn't laugh or anything at the thought of John being cool, too. Maybe I'm finally getting to her. I knew I could do it!

"Hey, Jensen," said a quiet voice next to me in study hall. It was Albert Causley.

"My friends call me Jellimiah," I said in my cool voice.

"I'm sure they do," Albert replied, fiddling with his black drawing pen. "But I call you Jensen," he added, his blue eyes narrowing at some private joke. Then he bowed his head, opened his sketchpad, and started drawing.

"Can I see?" I asked.

"Some other time, Jensen," he replied, still drawing.

A weird kid, I decided, and began thinking some more about Sondra and Missy. Missy likes John, but just as a friend. As usual, John loses out to the other guy. But Sondra likes Jellimiah. She *really* likes him. If only I could get her to transfer her interest to John. But something tells me John would never be Sondra's kind of guy. And, come to think of it, Sondra would never be John's kind of girl.

I was still thinking this through at three o'clock. I hadn't come to any major decisions about it. But I *had* decided that Jellimiah hadn't been sufficiently evil today. Sure, I'd flunked a math quiz and talked back to Mr. Trotter and Miss Thompson. But that wasn't enough.

As I headed down the hall, passing Cindi, who had her little nose in her locker, out of the corner of my eye I noticed the custodian step into a utility closet. And I noticed he'd left the key in the lock.

What I was thinking about doing wasn't nice, that was for sure. But it wasn't *that* awful. At least I hoped it wasn't. And I sure hoped he wasn't claustrophobic or anything like that. But he wouldn't be in there long. I wasn't going to be *that* evil!

In a flash I'd slammed the closet door and locked it.

"Hey! Let me outta here!" the custodian cried, and started banging on the door. When he found it was locked, he got so enraged I thought he was going to pound his way right through the door.

I took the key and headed nonchalantly down the hallway.

But the knocking and pounding and shouting had attracted attention.

"Is someone trapped in there?" inquired Cindi, looking around nervously.

"Maybe," I said with a smirk.

"He could suffocate," cried Cindi.

"Who cares?" I said. "I don't like custodians."

With that I headed off down the hall. My plan was to drop the key on the desk of Ms. Betterton, Miss Thompson's secretary. I didn't want anyone to suffocate, of course. I just wanted to be evil. And I wanted everyone to know I was evil. And I could count on Cindi telling everyone all about it.

But what I hadn't counted on was Cindi Greenbottom losing her mind.

"The custodian's dead!" she shrieked, tugging at the locked door. Then she began running in small circles in the hall, gasping for air as she circled. "Dead! Dead! Dead!" she yelped. "Suffocated in the closet and he can't get out!"

Soon a crowd had gathered.

I lingered just around the corner. I could peek and see them, but they couldn't see me. Before I dropped off the key, I wanted to see what happened. I knew it was a big enough closet, and the custodian would be all right for a while.

"Jellimiah just shoved the custodian in the closet!" shrieked Cindi.

"Cool!" said Jake. "I wish *I'd* thought of doing that."

"Jellimiah's so neat," enthused Sondra. "You never know what he's going to do next."

Missy and her boyfriend, Nick, soon joined the crowd. I saw Missy shake her head. *Well, who cares if she doesn't like Jellimiah?* I said to myself. I thought Nick looked slightly amused, but I couldn't tell for sure.

"Listen," said Missy, "we've got to get this poor guy out."

"I think he's already dead," said Cindi, still hyperventilating.

"But he's pounding against the door and shouting," Nick pointed out.

Clip-clop, clip-clop, clip-clop sounded from the far end of the hall.

"What in heaven's name is going on here?" demanded the shrill voice of Miss Thompson.

"Jellimiah locked the custodian in the closet!" gasped Cindi.

"Well, I never!" said Miss Thompson. "That boy is no good! I am going to have to talk with his mother and I'm going to speak with the superintendent and then I'm going to get his full record from California and then—"

"Miss Thompson," interrupted Nick, "why don't you make your plans later and get the custodian out now?"

"Good point, Nick," said Miss Thompson, her nostrils starting to quiver. And from halfway down the hall *and* around a corner, I could see the vein in her neck throbbing scarily.

"Whip," said Miss Thompson, "be a good boy and run to my office for the master key. I don't have it on me."

"I'll be quick," Whip said, and jogged off.

"Oh, why can't Jellimiah be more like his twin brother?" cried Miss Thompson. "Why, why, why?" Then she put her mouth up against the closet door and shrieked, "Don't despair, Mr. Robinson—we shall get you out!"

Soon Whip came running back and handed Miss Thompson the key.

"Never fear, Mr. Robinson," shouted Miss Thompson, fitting the key into the lock. "Help is at hand."

In another second the closet door was unlocked. It came flying open so quickly that Miss Thompson didn't have time to clip-clop out of the way. She was knocked off her high heels by the thick metal door. She gave a shriek and toppled over like a gangly giraffe—right up against little Cindi Greenbottom. Cindi crumpled beneath the unexpected weight and fell to the floor. Miss Thompson fell right on top of her. Poor Cindi was hyperventilating so loudly she sounded like an electric generator.

The custodian meanwhile had burst out of the closet. He didn't thank Miss Thompson for rescuing him. He didn't extract the squashed Cindi from under her. Instead, he charged off down the hall like a bat out of hell. At the far end, he darted through the door to the outside and disappeared.

"Poor Mr. Robinson," said Miss Thompson as she struggled to her feet. "He must have had a desperate need for fresh air!"

Missy and Nick pulled Cindi up from the floor and tried to calm her down.

Just then another custodian came trotting up. He and Miss Thompson began an intense discussion that looked like it was going to be tedious. So I stepped outside and counted to seventy-nine. I always count to seventy-nine. It gives me time to think, but not too much.

Okay, I thought, *now I'll saunter back. I can deny I ever did it. I can say Cindi got confused. That seems believable. They won't be able to suspend me. I'll just get yelled at.* I don't want to get suspended. I mean, if I can't go to school, then I can't have fun being evil—and I can't convince everyone to like John.

I got to seventy-nine and sauntered back in. I was bracing myself for the terrible sounds of Miss Thompson's shrieks and Cindi's hyperventilation.

"Jellimiah!" cried Cindi through her gasps. "You're a hero!"

"I didn't do it—" I began. "What did you say?" I asked.

"You're a hero!" cried Cindi again, and she threw her tiny arms around me.

"Way cool," said Jake.

"Neat!" cooed Sondra.

"Not bad," agreed Missy, nodding her head.

"What?" I cried. "But I—"

"If only I hadn't opened that door!" moaned Miss Thompson.

"What?"

"Yeah," agreed the custodian. "That was no custodian. I'm the only one on duty from one to nine. That guy was a fake."

"I suspect he was none other than the same person who tricked your dear brother on Friday," explained Miss Thompson. "Doubtless you recognized him from John's description. How clever you were to lock him in the closet! And how clever not to tell Cindi the reason why—you didn't want to set off a widespread panic. And then I hear you headed off in the direction of my office. Oh, if only I'd been there, we might have captured the thief before he could strike again!"

"But—"

"Remember," gasped Cindi, "I've got sixteen dollars and twenty-eight cents on me. I'm lucky he didn't grab that, too!"

"Do you have the key you locked him in with?" asked the real Mr. Robinson.

I took it out of my pocket and handed it to him.

"Hmm," he said. "It's a copy of the master key to the school."

"But only I have a master key!" exclaimed Miss Thompson.

"Not anymore," said Mr. Robinson.

"Then we're not safe!" Cindi yelped.

"Wait till my dad hears about this," said Sondra. "He'll sue the pants off everybody, and twice, too!"

"Now, now, Sondra, we mustn't overreact," cried Miss Thompson, her nostrils quivering madly and her neck vein bulging massively. Talk about not overreacting!

"We'll have to change all the locks," observed Mr. Robinson.

"But that'll cost a fortune!" moaned Miss Thompson, so sadly I almost felt sorry for her. "However shall I explain it to the school board?"

"Maybe you're all right after all," Missy said to me as she and Nick headed off.

I meant to be evil, but I ended up being a hero. Oh, well. But at least I impressed Missy.

Not to mention Sondra.

"Oh, Jellimiah," she cooed, "you were *so* brave!"

"It was nothing," I said.

And for once Jellimiah Jensen was telling the truth!

Tuesday, September 11, seventh period

My shirt was ironed and buttoned to the top. My pants were perfectly pressed. And my hair was neatly parted and patted down flat. As I left this morning, I looked at my Jellimiah clothing heaped on a chair in the corner of the room. I sure felt like wearing them again today. Let's face it: I have more fun being Jellimiah. Somehow I can say anything and do anything. And somehow I seem to get away with it. Being John can be a drag. I have to change that.

Maybe I *am* changing it a bit—didn't Sondra listen when Jellimiah told her John was really pretty cool? I decided on my way to school that today was the day when everyone at Edgewood Junior High would start liking John as much as they seem to like Jellimiah.

But the only person in homeroom who seemed happy to see me was Mr. Sterling.

"Good to see you, John," he said. "Is it your turn to come to school today?"

"Ah, Jellimiah had to go, um, meet with someone. I don't want to talk about it. It's personal."

"I don't suppose he gave you those excuses your parents wrote?" asked Mr. Sterling.

"I—I mean, we—we only have a mother," I replied kind of coldly. Aren't teachers supposed to be up on our family backgrounds? He should have known I'm from a single-parent family. "And no," I continued, "Jellimiah has them, but he didn't give them to me."

"What an irresponsible boy," said Mr. Sterling, shaking his head.

Sondra was ignoring me, but I noticed Whip trying to catch my eye.

"Is your brother okay?" he whispered.

"Sure," I said. "He just had to go meet with—"

"I heard you," Whip interrupted. "It wasn't about his ligament, was it?"

I wish Whip would ask me something about *me* sometimes. But it's always about Jellimiah. If I were Jellimiah today, I'd do something about it. But that just isn't the kind of thing John does.

At least not yet.

Anyway, I managed to get near Sondra on the way to first period. She was looking right at me. Then she opened her mouth. I could hardly believe it—she was going to speak to me! I held on tight to my notebook.

"Hey, jerk," she said, "gonna steal some more computers today?"

Then she gave a nasty giggle and went off in search of her friend Val.

I thought I was making progress. I really thought she was

starting to like me! Speaking of liking, I have to admit I'm starting to wonder why I like her so much.

"Sit down and quiet up," barked Mr. Trotter as we noisily entered math class. "I've got the results of our first quiz."

"I'm so nervous!" twittered Cindi. "I've got to get an A. I've just got to!"

"I gotta get a C," said Whip. "I gotta. Or else it's good-bye Panthers."

"I'm going to read the results aloud instead of returning them," announced Mr. Trotter.

"Aloud!" gasped Cindi, starting to breathe rapidly. "But that's not nice! Grades should be private! I don't want—"

"You got an A," interrupted Mr. Trotter, and started going down the class list, reading off grades as he went.

". . . Nanci Hester, C-plus; Anthony Isherwell, D-plus; Jellimiah Jensen—"

Here Mr. Trotter looked up, an odd expression on his face. He saw me looking at him. *Yes,* I thought, *he's going to have to give Jellimiah an F, or maybe even a zero!*

"Where's your brother?" asked Mr. Trotter.

"It's personal," I said, trying to act as though I were covering something up.

"Well, just as long as it isn't medical," replied Mr. Trotter. "You can tell your brother his grade. Jellimiah Jensen: B-plus."

"B-plus!" I gasped so loudly that Cindi Greenbottom fell off her chair.

"That's correct," said Mr. Trotter. "Now, where was I? John Jensen, absent; Bea Lehmann, B-minus; Lisa Merton, A-minus . . ."

My mouth dropped open. How could Jellimiah have gotten a B+? Had I somehow managed to make twenty lucky guesses? Only Jellimiah could be *that* lucky, I thought, starting to feel a little jealous all over again.

I was still thinking about it as Mr. Trotter continued down the list. ". . . James Van Der Plas, C-plus; Ralph Wypikowski—"

Whip sat up at attention. His thick neck was taut with anticipation.

"B-minus," said Mr. Trotter, and Whip heaved a sigh of relief.

Next period was science. Classes are being held in a conference room until the lab can be repaired. Mr. Fishwell doesn't like that one bit, and today he was even grumpier than usual. He made Cindi cry and he yelled six times at Jake for no reason at all. I guess he's having a bad day. Or maybe a bad year!

But one thing made Mr. Fishwell happy. Really happy.

In fact, he interrupted his lecture about the dangers of failing seventh-grade science (we'd never get into the college of our parents' choice) to say, "Well, gang, at least *one* good thing's happened today."

"What's that?" asked Cindi, brushing a tiny tear from the corner of her eye.

"Jellimiah Jensen's absent again," chuckled Mr. Fishwell. Then he returned to his lecture.

I didn't like that.

It isn't right.

Not at all.

Maybe teachers can't like every single kid they teach, but they shouldn't announce it to the class.

I was going to say something out loud about it, but I didn't.

That would be a Jellimiah thing to do, not a John thing.

I was feeling kind of nervous when English rolled around. What if Mr. Forester held a grudge? I really want him to like me.

The second I entered the room he took me aside. I saw Missy watching us. I wondered what she was thinking.

Here it comes, I thought. *The lecture. How he's disappointed in me. How he hopes next time I'll look before I leap. Et cetera, et cetera.*

But he just slapped me on the back and smiled.

"We won't say another word about it," he said gently. "Okay?"

"Okay," I said, and headed happily to find a seat.

Nick was already sitting next to Missy. They were so busy chatting they didn't even notice me as I went by. I figured they were talking about what a major moron I was to steal those computers and what a hero Jellimiah was to almost capture the burglar.

"I've got a surprise," said Mr. Forester.

We looked up expectantly.

"Mr. Siegel over in the computer lab said we could use his machines for our literary magazine until we get ours replaced. Nick's already written software to save everything we produce and store it separately. We don't want anything getting lost by mistake. A lot of other groups use Mr. Siegel's equipment, and some of them might not be as computer-literate as I know all of you are."

"Are we going there right now?" asked Cindi, who was still a bit teary-eyed from science class and Mr. Fishwell.

"Yep," said Mr. Forester. "Let's go."

Missy kind of smiled at me on the way to the computer lab, but no one else paid much attention to me except for Albert and Cindi. But all Albert did was nod in my direction and go on walking in his dreamy way. And all Cindi wanted to talk about was the burglary. And that was something I, for one, wanted to forget all about!

"You can just play around today if you want to," said Mr.

Forester when we'd arrived in the lab. "I want you to get used to the machines. But if you write something worth saving and you make a printout for yourself, thanks to Nick's system it will be properly saved."

"What's Nick," I asked Cindi, "a computer genius or something?"

"He's the smartest guy in the seventh grade," answered Cindi, "except maybe for Albert."

"Oh," I said. No wonder Missy likes him so much. I bet he's a good writer, too. Anyway, that just made me more determined to write something totally excellent for our class's literary magazine. And I had to write something to-tally *un*excellent as Jellimiah, so Missy will like John more!

As the class settled down, my fingers hovered over the keyboard. Even though I was John today, I just wasn't in the mood to write anything excellent. So I decided to write something really stupid for Jellimiah.

I got to work.

Soon I sat back and looked at what I'd written on the computer screen. I'd turned off the spell-check, so it was *truly* pathetic.

Here's what I created:

Date: Tuesday, September 11
Class: Honors English
Teacher: Mr. Forester
Student: J. Jensen

"MOVEING"

I uset to live on the west coste but then I moved. Now I live on the east coste. Its diferrent from the west coste in lots of diferrent ways. But its kind of the same

64

to. Becauze on both costes their is a lot of water. Thats why their costes—their on the water.

Another diferrence is I uset to live in California but now I live in New York. One of them is bigger but I forget wich. I think California but Im not shure.

I also go to a diferrent skool. Its grose. And thats what its like to move.

THE END

I made myself a printout and almost laughed out loud as I read it. It was the worst thing I've ever seen! If Missy likes Nick because he's such a brain, well, she certainly won't like Jellimiah after she reads that! And maybe, somehow, she'll end up liking me once I write something amazing.

Some other kids had also gotten down to writing. I saw Cindi tapping at the keyboard a mile a minute. Maybe she was writing about hyperventilating. Missy was also hard at work. I peered at her screen. It looked as though she was composing a poem, probably about Nick. Nick himself was also working at a rapid pace. I never saw anyone type so fast. Maybe when he grows he'll be a secretary. Albert was just staring at his computer. It didn't look as though he likes computers very much.

Anyway, it was later on when I was on my way to gym class that I saw him.

Or maybe I should say, that was when I *didn't* see him. I'd better explain.

I was heading down the hallway, walking all alone, when I saw a man dip into a utility closet. He was dressed in a custodian's uniform, but even though I didn't get a good look at his face, from behind I could tell it wasn't Mr. Robinson. This guy was a lot taller. In fact, he was the same height as the guy I helped steal the computers last Friday. I also remembered that Mr. Robinson was the only custodian on duty from one to nine, and it was now two-fifteen.

I could hardly believe it—that fool burglar had come back! Instantly I got a great idea. Not only was I going to get him back for tricking me into stealing Mr. Forester's computers, I was going to make John Jensen as big a hero as Jellimiah. No, he'd be bigger, 'cause he'd actually catch the burglar!

I raced over and slammed the door on the surprised burglar.

"Hey!" he shouted. "Let me outta here!"

"Never!" I answered. "You won't escape this time!"

"What the—" began the burglar, but I ignored him.

"What's going on here?" asked Señora Gonzales as she passed me in the hallway.

"I've trapped the burglar!" I cried. "Quick! Get Miss Thompson! Hurry!"

Señora Gonzales ducked into a classroom and called the front office.

Clip-clop, clip-clop soon sounded in the hallway, and a breathless Miss Thompson came trotting up to me.

"John, you dear boy—is it true? Have you captured the criminal!"

I nodded and pointed proudly to the closet. "He's in there," I boasted.

"And just hear how furious he is!" cried Miss Thompson, listening to the shouts, hollers, and pounding issuing from the closet.

I was happy to see that a small crowd had gathered. Sondra was there. Missy, too. Almost every kid I knew was there, plus many I didn't. I was going to have my moment in the sun! John Jensen—hero!

All eyes were on me as Miss Thompson went to unlock the closet. Whip, Jake, Nick, and some others formed a semicircle around the closet so the burglar couldn't make a run for it like last time.

"Shouldn't we wait for the police?" worried Cindi. "What if he's armed and dangerous?"

"I could tackle him," promised Whip.

"Get ready!" I called as Miss Thompson opened the closet door.

An angry man charged out. He looked ready to punch me in the nose. "We've got you now," I said, trying to act cool. I was thinking to myself how clever he was—he'd even managed to get an Edgewood Junior High custodial staff uniform. He didn't look exactly the way I remembered him, but when I was assisting him load the van, I was so busy thinking about how wonderfully helpful I was being that I didn't really notice what he looked like.

But I did notice the expressions on the faces of Miss Thompson and all the kids standing around the closet.

Sondra gave a nasty giggle and poked Val, who started giggling, too.

"He's just trying to copy his brother," Sondra sneered.

"Yeah," agreed Val, "but look at what the clod caught!"

Missy and Nick looked embarrassed. Cindi looked troubled. Whip looked like he was trying to figure out a difficult math problem. And Albert just looked amused. Only Jake seemed impressed.

"Way cool!" he said. "Let's lock up all the custodians!"

"But he's not—" I began, when Miss Thompson tapped me lightly on the shoulder.

"John," she said, "I guess you haven't met Mr. Ford—one of our custodians."

"B-But . . . but Mr. Robinson said he was the only one who worked from one till nine," I stammered.

"Yeah, but not on Tuesdays," said Mr. Ford. "*I* work on Tuesdays."

"Oh," I said as Mr. Ford stomped off down the hall, shaking his head.

Miss Thompson ran after him, trying to soothe his nerves and explain what had happened.

Missy shot me a pitying look as she and Nick headed to class. They were followed by Jake, Whip, and Cindi. For once Cindi wasn't hyperventilating.

"What a superdweeb!" mocked Sondra as she and Val walked away.

"That's for sure," agreed Val. "He's off the A-list, right?"

"*He* was never on it," laughed Sondra. "But his brother sure is! There's no one like Jellimiah—no one!"

∾

Wednesday, September 12, third period

"Aren't you going to the hospital?" I asked Mom this morning.

"I can go in an hour late today," she said with a smile. "For once we can have a relaxed breakfast together, then I can drive you to school. Maybe you'd even have time to show me around a bit."

I gulped. I hadn't counted on this bit of maternal interest. I mean, Mom's really interested in my life and all. But usually she's so busy at the hospital that she doesn't have much time left over to wonder about what's going on at school.

I had to keep her away from Edgewood Junior High! What if Miss Thompson came clip-clopping over and wanted to talk about Jellimiah?

I had to think fast.

"Uh, gosh, Mom," I said, "I wish you'd told me earlier. I only have time for a quick breakfast with you. Then, um,

I'm meeting some kids to, um, discuss some work we're doing for our, um, class literary magazine."

"You should have invited them to the house," said Mom, putting some butter and jam on her roll. "I'd love to meet your new friends."

My new friends, I thought. *I don't have any yet.* Only Jellimiah has friends. Well, maybe Missy likes me a little, but she'll probably change her mind after yesterday, when I locked the custodian in the closet. But everyone else sure seems to like Jellimiah better.

Jellimiah! I suddenly wondered how on earth I was going to be Jellimiah today the way I wanted to be. Neat, normal John couldn't leave the house in rags and big boots, and since the clothes and boots wouldn't fit in my backpack with my school stuff, I'd have to cram some of it into another bag, and Mom would certainly want to know what was in it.

I was so busy thinking that I suddenly realized Mom was talking.

". . . and I'm planning on getting more involved with Edgewood Junior High," she was saying.

"But Mom—"

"We're in a new town and you're in a new school. I *am* busy at the hospital, but I'm going to find time to spend an hour or two at your new school, just to get to know it a bit."

"You don't want to know it," I argued. "I mean, it's a terrible place! The principal's a total lunatic, and the science teacher is incredibly mean, and—"

"Oh, John," Mom interrupted, "when you exaggerate like that you really remind me of my father. Maybe I should start calling you Jellimiah again!"

I just shook my head.

"Well," continued Mom after she'd taken a sip of coffee, "can I drive you to where you're meeting your friends?"

"Meeting my friends?"

"You just said you were meeting your friends."

"Oh, them," I said quickly. "Um, no, it's only around the corner. I don't need a lift. But thanks," I added as I got up to go.

"All right, dear," said Mom. "Have a nice day. Bye!"

"Bye, Mom," I said, and left the house—in my John clothes.

I didn't want to go to school as John, though. I wanted to be Jellimiah today because I want to have lunch with Sondra again. I mean, she *is* the prettiest and most popular girl in the seventh grade, even if she is kind of a snob. *Kind* of a snob? She's a *major* snob. I hate to admit it, but I am really having doubts about Sondra. But I still want to have lunch with her. I can't help it. And the only way she'll eat with me is if I'm Jellimiah.

So after I left the house this morning, I hid behind the garage. My plan was to wait until Mom left for the hospital and then change into my Jellimiah clothes. It meant I would be late, but I didn't care.

I was kind of surprised that I *didn't* care about being late—that's not like me. It's more like Jellimiah. Anyway, as I was sitting behind the garage I started thinking about John and Jellimiah . . . Jellimiah and John. I know I can't keep on being twins past the end of this week. Someone's sure to catch on. It's amazing no one has figured it out yet.

As I waited for Mom's car to pull out of the driveway I started to try to figure out how to get rid of my evil twin. Soon I realized it'd be harder than I thought. I mean, I *like* Jellimiah. It would be like getting rid of a real person.

Then another possibility occurred to me: Maybe I don't

have to get rid of Jellimiah. Maybe I can get rid of John! Why not? I can do it. I can become Jellimiah if I want!

Anyway, I thought about this all the way to school. Still wondering who I should become, I clomped into my first-period class, history. I was twenty-five minutes late. Mr. Morris, the teacher, sent me to the office for a late pass.

Miss Thompson seemed to be waiting for me. She was rubbing her long fingers together and her nostrils were just beginning to quiver.

"Skipping first period, were we?" she asked with a terrible smile.

"Nah," I said, "I just, ah, didn't feel too well when I woke up this morning. I thought I had a bug or something. John was *really* feeling sick. So I thought maybe I had it, too. Twins often get sick at the same time, you know. I was going to stay home, but then I started feeling okay, so I came to school."

"I see," said Miss Thompson. "Jellimiah, I'll have you know I just telephoned your house when I received a report that both you and John were absent from homeroom *and* first period. And no one answered!"

"So?" I said. "I'm here. My mom's at work. Why should anyone answer?"

"I'm talking about your dear brother!" cried Miss Thompson. "How could you forget about him?"

"Oh," I said. "John. He *is* kind of forgettable, you know."

The vein in Miss Thompson's neck started throbbing. "You just told me John was ill! And he's home alone! And he didn't answer the phone! What if he's taken a turn for the worse?"

"Oh, John's fine," I said. "He's probably just napping. Whenever John feels sick he sleeps like a log. He doesn't even answer the phone."

Miss Thompson shook her head. "I am deeply concerned," she said. "Deeply. You two boys are absent so frequently! John has that trouble with his wrist and Mr. Trotter tells me that you have a sprained ligament in your leg. I am worried. Especially about dear John. And I shall not stop worrying until I have reached him on the phone and heard his voice!"

"Well," I said, "I'll, um, give him a call later on and tell him to phone you."

"But," cried Miss Thompson, "you said dear John doesn't answer the phone when he's ill."

"He'll answer if *I* call," I boasted.

"But how will he know it's you?"

"How will he know it's me?" I repeated, wondering about that myself. "Well," I began, starting to wish I'd never been twins, "well—"

"I know!" cried Miss Thompson suddenly. "Of course! It's so obvious!"

"It is?" I said. "I mean, it *is*."

"Yes," said Miss Thompson with another of her terrible smiles, "I've read about there being mental telepathy between twins. Surely John can sense it is you on the phone, so he'll pick up because he already knows it's you. Am I right?"

"Right as rain," I said, wondering where that silly expression came from.

"Nonetheless," continued Miss Thompson, the terrible smile falling from her lips, "I still must speak directly with your mother about the fact that you have neglected to bring in excuses concerning your and your brother's absences. It's the sixth day of school and both you and John have been absent three times each."

"We're kind of sickly," I said.

"You do not look it," said Miss Thompson, "but I shall have to talk to your mother about it. And, furthermore, I mean to talk to her about your rudeness to your teachers. Jellimiah, I have already received a note about you from Mr. Fishwell. He even expressed the wish to have you transferred out of his class."

"That old turkey!"

"That," said Miss Thompson, "is precisely the kind of rudeness I am sure Mr. Fishwell finds so insupportable."

"He just doesn't like the way I look," I insisted.

"Really, Jellimiah," snorted Miss Thompson, "your garb, while unusual, is not something with which Mr. Fishwell would concern himself. It is your attitude. It is this I wish to discuss with your mother. I shall call her this very day."

"But she's very busy at the hospital," I said. "She can't even answer phone calls. She's a surgeon, you know. You wouldn't want to interrupt her while she's taking out someone's appendix, would you?"

"I am quite aware of your mother's profession," sniffed Miss Thompson. "She shall come to the phone when I call. I am Miss Thompson."

Just then the intercom buzzed. It was Miss Thompson's secretary. "There's a phone call for you," came Ms. Betterton's voice over the intercom. "It's Ms. Nolan."

"Oh, merciful heavens!" cried Miss Thompson, her nostrils going wild. "She's the president of the school board! Whatever will I tell her?"

"Tell her you quit," I mumbled.

"What did you say?" demanded Miss Thompson.

"I said, um, tell her she's a nitwit."

"I wish I could," sighed Miss Thompson. And for the first time since I've known her, she gave me a real smile, not a terrible one. But it didn't last long. "You are dismissed," she said, handing me a late pass. "Make sure your brother calls me. And if you speak with your mother during the day, make sure she calls me as well." Then she picked up the phone. "Ms. Nolan," she said in a sugary voice, "what a sweet surprise. Perhaps you're calling about that little mix-up with the master key? Well . . ."

I made my way back to history. I was so preoccupied that I forgot to thump as I walked. What if Miss Thompson reached Mom? I had to stop her! I had to!

I passed Albert in the hall, just standing there.

"Hey, Jensen," he said.

"I'm *Jellimiah*," I reminded him.

Albert ignored my remark.

"You know what?" he said. "I never told you this before, but I'm a twin."

"But Miss Thompson said I was the only twin in the seventh grade." Whoops! I should have said "we."

"That's because my twin brother goes to private school," explained Albert. "Our parents thought it was better for us to go to separate schools. So," he continued, "I know a lot about twins. A *lot*."

"That's nice," I said, running my hand through my moussed hair to cover up the fact that I was feeling a bit nervous.

"And," added Albert, "how can I put it—I know it can be hard to be a twin. Especially—"

"Especially in a new school," I interrupted, and headed back to history.

After giving Mr. Morris my late pass, I sat down and thought. How on earth could I prevent Miss Thompson from calling Mom? There had to be a way to stall her until I stop being twins. Today is Wednesday, so it would be only three more days, counting today. Then Jellimiah—or John!—will vanish.

I thought about stopping my twins routine tomorrow, but I don't think I'm ready yet. After all, I haven't decided which one I want to be. So I had to come up with something. I could just imagine what would happen if Miss Thompson got a hold of Mom—I'd be suspended *and* grounded! What a combination! But I was cornered, and the more I tried to think, the less I could figure out. I sat there wishing I'd never met nosy Miss Thompson.

Then, out of the blue, I got a brainstorm.

Yes!

I raised my hand and got permission to use the bathroom. I headed straight for a pay phone.

"Miss Thompson," I was soon saying, "it's John Jensen."

"John!" cried Miss Thompson. "I'd know your voice anywhere—it's so unlike your brother's! How are you feeling?"

"All right, I guess," I said. "Better than I felt this morning."

"I am delighted to hear it," said Miss Thompson. "I've been so concerned—which is more than I can say for your brother. In fact, he almost appeared to forget he even had a brother! Most shocking!"

"Oh, Jellimiah's not so bad," I said in case I end up becoming him full time. "I bet you'd like him if you got to know him."

"What a generous boy you are!" enthused Miss Thompson. "But really, John, I doubt even Jellimiah's own mother would find him likable."

"Speaking of mothers," I said, grabbing my chance, "Jellimiah mentioned you wanted to speak to my mom."

"Yes, I feel it is my—"

"Please don't," I interrupted. I had to get off the phone

76

before some noise near the pay phone could alert Miss Thompson that I was phoning from school.

"Whyever not?"

This was where my brainstorm came in. "It's like this," I explained. "My mom gets upset whenever people bring up Jellimiah. She's worried about him herself. If she hears other people are worried, too, then she gets even more worried. And when she gets worried, I get worried. And when I get worried, I get sick even more often. I might end up being absent for weeks and weeks!"

"But John—" began Miss Thompson. Just then I saw Jake clumping up in his oversize Jellimiah boots. I knew he was bound to shout a loud greeting.

"I've got to go, Miss Thompson," I said hurriedly. "I'm, um, feeling faint. Just promise me you won't worry my mom about Jellimiah!"

"I promise—" Miss Thompson was saying as I hung up.

And in the nick of time, too.

At that very moment Jake roared out, "Hey there, Jellimiah—what's up?"

By the time I got back to history, the period was almost over. When the bell rang, I got up and shuffled over to math class. Mr. Trotter was so happy to see me he almost fell over. "How's our star quarterback?" he wanted to know. "That ligament all healed?"

"It's okay, but not all better."

"Well, make sure it gets better."

"Uh-huh," I said nonchalantly. I don't like Mr. Trotter. He isn't nice to me when I'm John.

"You got your quiz results from your brother?" asked Mr. Trotter.

I nodded.

"Good," said Mr. Trotter. "We'll make sure you keep up the good work."

Then he winked.

And then I knew how I'd gotten that B+.

It wasn't Jellimiah's dumb luck. It was Mr. Trotter. What a crook! And what an idiot I've been not to have guessed it right away. It makes me want to expose Mr. Trotter if it's the last thing I do.

"Sit down, class," continued Mr. Trotter in a more formal voice. "We've got a pop quiz today."

This time it wasn't multiple choice. We had to do calculations and come up with the answers ourselves. Good. I could *really* screw this one up! I whipped through it, writing down the most outlandish numbers: $52\frac{1}{3}$ for the first answer, -6,428.62 for the second. No way I can get a B+. No way! With answers like that, Mr. Trotter can't possibly give me good grades I don't deserve just to get me on the Panthers!

I have to smile, though, when I think about how surprised he'd be if he did get me on the Panthers and I showed up and played as badly as I always do. He'd die! It almost seems worth doing, except I know it would make me look like a total turkey.

But that raises another problem. What would I do about football if I end up staying Jellimiah? How could I avoid trying out? I guess I could always claim my ligament still isn't healed.

And then there's Whip. In math class today, during the quiz, I sneaked a look at his paper while he was hard at work on the first question. I did it in my head and waited to see what answer he'd come up with.

He noticed me looking at him and nodded in my direction.

I looked away, then looked back.

Whip nodded at me again and wrote down an answer.

It was wrong. Way wrong.

That made me feel kind of bad for him. I know he can't be maintaining a C average, and if I expose Mr. Trotter, then Whip might end up being kicked off the football team. That would break his heart. And even if he does kind of ignore me when I'm John, I still think he's an all-right kind of guy.

Now I *really* don't know what to do.

Wednesday, September 12, after school

"Your brother, John, is *such* a dweeb," Sondra was saying over lunch. "I thought I'd die when he locked Mr. Ford in the closet yesterday! All he was doing was trying to be as cool as you are. He might as well just forget it!"

"Nah," I said, "you've got it all wrong. John is a great guy. Really."

"Do you know what the day after tomorrow is?" asked Sondra, quickly changing the subject.

"Sure. It's Friday."

Sondra smiled and looked around. It was a sunny day and we were sitting alone on the terrace outside the cafeteria. Other kids were at other tables, but no one was with us. Even Val wasn't there. I liked that. Sondra wanted to be alone with me. Yes!

Too bad I have such doubts about her.

"It's not just Friday," Sondra said. "It's also the day of the First Party."

"What do you mean, the First Party?" I asked as I fiddled with a stalk of celery.

"It's, like, an Edgewood custom. Every September the head cheerleader for each grade—that's me, of course—gives a party at her house for the entire grade."

"Whoa!" I said, running my hand through my moussed hair. "That must be one big party."

Sondra gave another smile and looked over her shoulder before speaking.

"You're right, Jellimiah," she said, "it *is* kind of big for one party. So we started a tradition of giving two—one this Friday, one next Friday."

"How do you figure out who comes to which party?" I asked.

"It's *supposed* to be a lottery," said Sondra in a low voice. "You see, the whole point of the party is for the kids in each grade to get together and have fun and be friendly and all that stuff. Like *I'd* ever want to be friendly with the dorks and the dweebs and the brains! They are major uncool!"

I gulped. I almost snapped my celery stalk in two. That's who I was in my last school. A dork. A dweeb. A brain. Major uncool.

"So," I asked, "how *do* you divide up the grade?"

"Val and I were up until midnight last night," said Sondra. "But we finally finished making up an A-list and a B-list. The A-list is all the cool kids and the B-list is the dweebs. And it's so neat! The student council gives the party-giver a budget for the parties. Well, Val and I have ordered all the food and soda, and we're spending eighty percent of the budget for the A-list party and twenty percent for the dorks. So the cool kids will have a cool time and the dweebs won't even know the difference. They've probably never been to a party in their whole lives anyway."

"But won't somebody notice that the kids you like are going to one party and everyone else is going to the other?"

Sondra shook her head and beamed. "Val and I thought of that, too. You see, we invited a few of the dorks to the good party. And a few of my friends, like Val, volunteered to go to the dork party, too. That way the dweebs see a few cool kids at their party and they feel cool, too. Is that neat or what?"

I nodded. But it didn't sound neat. Not at all. It sounded bogus. I remembered all the parties I hadn't been invited to in Los Angeles because someone didn't think I was cool enough.

Why do I still like Sondra, anyway? Is it just because she's so pretty and popular? No, there has to be something more. But what is it?

"Anyway," Sondra was saying, "we're supposed to give out all the invitations today, during seventh period. We even get to go into classes and do it. Will you help?"

"Uh, sure," I said. "I guess."

"Oh, Jellimiah, you are such a doll!" gushed Sondra. And she leaned across the table and gave me a kiss. It was a nice kiss. "I'm glad you agreed to help! It's fun handing out the invitations. Kids act so thrilled to get them. It's supposed to make us into one happy bunch of kids who get along. Forget that! As if I'd even *want* to get along with jerks like that ugly hyperbrain Missy Einhorn!"

"She's on the B-list?"

"I'm just sorry I have to invite her at all," said Sondra.

Without even knowing I was doing it, I snapped my celery stalk into two pieces.

"So which party is my brother going to?" I wondered.

"Do you even have to ask?" said Sondra, snickering. "If there were a C-list, he'd be on it. I'm thinking of telling him to go to the wrong address!"

I dropped my pieces of celery.

I gulped. I saw red. I felt sad.

"Sondra," I said, "didn't it ever occur to you that since John is my brother, I might care about him?"

Sondra gave a little giggle.

"Don't be silly!" she said. "He's a dweeb and a brain. Yucky!"

I gulped again. I saw red again. And I felt even sadder. Then I got another of my brainstorms. I'm not my evil twin for nothing!

"Sondra," I said, "I won't help you after all."

"But—" began Sondra.

"No," I interrupted, "I'll do it all myself. You've, um, done enough already with all your planning and making lists and stuff. I've got a study hall seventh period today, so it'll be no sweat to give out the invitations all by myself."

"I *knew* you were a doll!" cooed Sondra. And she leaned over to kiss me again. I kind of pulled away, so Sondra ended up kissing the air. No one calls Missy ugly. And no one puts John on a C-list and sends him—I mean me!—to the wrong address! No one.

"When did you get so shy?" asked Sondra as she reached into her bag and handed me two stacks of invitations. "Anyway, this stack here with the red rubber band around it is the A-list. The one with the brown band is the dork pile. The kids' names are on the envelopes. All you have to do is hand them out," she added bossily. "Make sure no A-list invites get in the hands of B-list kids. I don't want B-list dorks coming to my A-list party." She eyed a nerd-girl named Regina Whitman trot by looking for a lost library book. "Especially Regina! Or the Welch cousins, Fred and Franklin!"

"Of course not," I mumbled, my thoughts far away by then.

"You are *so* cool, Jellimiah," cooed Sondra. "Wait till Val hears what you're doing for me," she added as she got up to leave. "She won't believe it."

"I can hardly believe it, either," I said.

With the two piles of invitations in a bag under my arm, I arrived in Mr. Fishwell's science class.

"Oh," said Mr. Fishwell when I thumped in, "it's you. Too bad. I was hoping it would be John. At any rate, you're late. Go get a late pass."

"But Mr. Fishwell," piped up Cindi, "Jellimiah's not late. Look—the late bell hasn't rung yet."

"Uh, right, Cindi," grunted Mr. Fishwell. "All right, what are you waiting for, Jensen? Sit down."

I smiled at Cindi as I found my seat. She smiled back.

Forgetting about Cindi, I focused on Mr. Fishwell's lecture. It was about the skeletal system. Since Mom's specialty is orthopedic surgery, I already know quite a bit about it. Probably even more than Mr. Fishwell.

When Mr. Fishwell had finished lecturing, he stopped for questions and comments. I was so intent on saying something that I forgot to be evil. I raised my arm so high it nearly came flying out of its socket. But Mr. Fishwell never called on me. Not even once. He'd just turn his pudgy face in a different direction every time he saw me raising my hand.

After Mr. Fishwell finished ignoring me, he announced we'd be spending the remainder of the class watching a video instead of performing the experiment we'd have been doing if we'd been in the lab (which is still under repair).

Producing his key, Mr. Fishwell went to a large cabinet where the VCR was stored. He unlocked the door and opened it.

"It's gone!" he shouted. "The VCR is gone! Stolen!"

For a moment Mr. Fishwell looked stunned. Then he pulled himself together. Then he glared at me.

"Jellimiah Jensen," he said sternly, "do *you* know anything about this?"

"Why should *I* know anything about it?" I demanded in my loud Jellimiah voice.

"Because," said Mr. Fishwell, "if the shoe fits, wear it."

"Jerk," I said, staring back at Mr. Fishwell's broad face.

"But Mr. Fishwell," Cindi suddenly gasped out (the news of another burglary had brought on another attack of hyperventilation), "don't you remember? It was Jellimiah who almost captured the burglar!"

"I suppose so," grumbled Mr. Fishwell as he made his way to the phone to alert Miss Thompson of the latest theft.

"You can all leave," he told us. "Go to study hall. I'm too upset to teach."

We made a mad dash for the door before he could change his mind.

"Jensen," he added as I'd almost made the hall, "I've still got my doubts about you."

"And I've got *my* doubts about *you*," I said with a smirk as I headed off.

My destination was the front office. I'd passed Miss Thompson clip-clopping rapidly toward Mr. Fishwell's room, so I knew the coast was clear: I could sneak by the secretary.

Yes! The copy machine was mine! It was a good thing it stood all alone in its own little room.

It only took six and a half minutes. I was out of there in time for my next class, English.

"I know a number of you began some writing last time that you'd like to continue today," Mr. Forester said to us once we'd assembled in Mr. Siegel's computer lab. "So grab a computer and get to work!"

I sat down at the computer right next to Missy's, beating out Nick by two seconds. He looked bugged, but that wasn't my fault. You have to be quick to beat out Jellimiah Jensen!

"Is John sick again?" asked Missy in a concerned voice. (How could Sondra say Missy is ugly?)

"Just a little," I said. "But he'll be back tomorrow."

"Good," said Missy.

I couldn't believe she said "Good"! My heart leaped, and I tried not to grin.

". . . how does that sound?" she was asking me.

I shook my head to clear it. "I'm sorry—what did you say?"

"I said, I think that's what I'm going to write my poem about," Missy repeated.

"Uh . . . sounds great," I replied, not having any idea what she was going to write about.

"Thanks, Jellimiah," said Missy as she got back to work. "Good luck with your writing!"

I needed luck, and a lot of it. I had to write something great for John. Something that would impress Missy. Something that would leave Nick in the dust. Something to make up for my stealing the computers, then locking the custodian in the closet.

I'd never thought I was good at making things up, so I decided not to write a story. And since Missy was working on a poem, I ruled out poetry. Then I realized I could write something factual, like an exposé—a hard-hitting report that would start me out on a career in journalism!

First I thought I'd expose Mr. Trotter. But then I remembered Whip. If I expose Mr. Trotter, chances are Whip will be tossed off the team, since he can't really have a C average in math. That doesn't seem fair. I mean, maybe he doesn't even bother to study math since he knows Mr. Trotter will give him C's no matter what.

But the more I thought about an exposé, the more I liked the idea—except for hurting Whip.

Then I got an idea. It was more like another brainstorm.

I got to work. I was inspired. And when I'm inspired, I work quickly. Thirty-six minutes later, I sat back and read through what I'd written.

Then I smiled at what was on the screen.

Even the heading looked good to me!

Here's how it began:

Date: Wednesday, September 12
Class: Honors English, 7th Grade
Teacher: Mr. Forester
Student: J. Jensen

"THE NEW BOY"

What I did was write a story about a new boy. Anyone reading it will know it's about Jellimiah, even though I gave him a different name. And anyone reading it will guess who "Mr. Gallop" is and who "Mr. Sharkwell" is. I told everything. Well, almost everything. I wrote about a math teacher who passes the new boy just because he thinks the kid is good at sports. And a science teacher who has it in for the new boy just because it was he who smelled gas, not the teacher himself. But it's not all bad. I wrote about a nice English teacher, "Mr. Orchard."

I think it's the best thing I've ever written.

And I don't think it'll get anyone in trouble. It'll just serve as a warning that I know what's going on.

I had just made a print-out when a voice asked, "What are you smiling about?" It was Missy.

"Oh, nothing," I said, trying to act modest.

"You look happy about what you wrote," observed Missy. "Can I read it?"

"No!" I shouted. Missy can't read it until John is back and can show it to her. I want her to think John wrote it.

"It's not so hot," I said finally. "But wait till you read what my brother wrote! Now *that's* worth reading!"

"I'm sure it is," said Missy. "John is . . . well . . ."

"Well what?" I asked.

"I think he's kind of special," said Missy, blushing a bit as she turned back to her computer.

She likes me!

Maybe she's getting tired of Nick after all. Maybe there's hope for me!

But what about Sondra? Well, Sondra Settle is in for a little Jellimiah-style surprise. Wait till she discovers what I did with her invitations during seventh period. She deserves it, even if she is the most popular girl at Edgewood Junior High.

You could say I'm a fool. If I dated the most popular girl in school, then I'd end up being the most popular boy. But when she finds out what I did, she'll never speak to Jellimiah again. And I'll have to stay John, that's for sure. You don't mess with the most popular girl in school.

But I still kind of want to stay Jellimiah. . . .

John or Jellimiah? Jellimiah or John? Who should I be?

Thursday, September 13, after school

Mom was so upset at breakfast this morning she poured orange juice on her cereal.

I waited. I know my mom. She doesn't like being rushed. I knew she'd tell me sooner or later what was on her mind. I thought maybe it had something to do with the hospital.

"John, dear," she said at last, "I'm really worried about something."

"What is it?" I asked.

Mom took a big gulp of coffee, then spoke.

"I'm thinking of withdrawing you from Edgewood and placing you in a private school," she announced.

"What?" I hollered.

"It's just . . . well, I feel uncomfortable having you in a school run by . . . run by . . ."

"Run by what?" I asked, still in a state of shock.

Mom sighed. "I hate to say this, dear, but I think you

were right about the principal. Your Miss Thompson is a lunatic. I'm not at all sure she should be working with young people."

I almost choked on my cereal.

"What makes you think Miss Thompson is a lunatic?"

"Well, I was on rounds yesterday afternoon and my beeper sounded. I called in for the message, and there was one from Miss Thompson. It said it was an emergency, and she was waiting on the line to speak with me. So of course I took the call. I was concerned something might have happened to you."

What a dirty double-crosser! Miss Thompson promised she wouldn't call Mom.

"Wh-what did she say?" I asked, afraid of the answer.

"I could barely make sense of it," Mom replied. "You see, I was speaking to her from a phone in a busy corridor—I didn't have time to find a phone in a quiet location. Anyway Miss Thompson said . . . she said . . ." Mom shook her head.

"What?"

"I must have misheard her," Mom finally said. "That's it. Or perhaps she had me confused with someone else. That's even more likely. Yes, I'm sure of it. It had to be a case of mistaken identity."

"But what did she say?" I persisted.

She hesitated for a moment, then said, "Since it was evidently a miscommunication of some sort, I don't think it would be fair for me to repeat our conversation. It makes Miss Thompson sound absolutely deranged."

"C'mon, Mom, tell me what she said," I begged.

"My lips are sealed," said Mom firmly. She began eating her soggy, orange-juice-flavored cereal. "I'm just glad that I didn't lose my temper with her the way she did with me."

I know my mom, and I knew she wouldn't tell me what happened, at least not for a good long while.

But something told me someone else would.

No sooner had I walked through the front door at Edgewood than I saw Miss Thompson waiting for me. Her nostrils were raging and her neck looked like a mountain range.

"John, dearest John," shrieked Miss Thompson so loudly that everyone heard, "we must speak. You, I, and Jellimiah. It's urgent. *Urgent!*"

"Jellimiah's absent," I mumbled.

"Again?" cried Miss Thompson. "What is the matter this time?"

"Um, it's still his ligament," I explained. "That old waterskiing injury. It's acting up again. He could barely walk when he woke up this morning."

"How unfortunate," remarked Miss Thompson as she directed me toward her office. "John," she continued in a softer voice once we'd arrived there and were seated in the two easy chairs in the corner of her office, "I am afraid I have something difficult to discuss."

"Oh?" I said, and waited.

Miss Thompson coughed and patted her hands nervously against the sides of her nose. I wondered if she was trying to discourage her nostrils from vibrating.

"I felt obliged to call your mother," she began. "I recall you asked me not to, John. Now I can see why. It's tragic. Utterly tragic."

"It is?" I said.

"I understand it all completely," said Miss Thompson in a concerned tone. "Perhaps I shouldn't discuss it with you, but I feel I must. It is quite evident that having a difficult child in the family has pushed your mother quite over the edge. When I brought up your brother, she sounded nearly like a lunatic."

Hmm, I thought. *And to think she said the same thing about you!*

"Yes," continued Miss Thompson, "it is no wonder you boys suffer from such ill health. It is surely a reaction to having such an unbalanced mother."

"She's not unbalanced," I said. "My mom's—"

"Hush, dear child," said Miss Thompson. "There is no need to protect your mother. I know all. I have spoken with her. I told her how concerned I was about the repeated absences of her two sons. And do you know what she said? She told me you were in perfect health and—this is ten times worse!—she claimed she has only one son. 'But Dr. Jensen,' I told her, 'you have two sons. Two!' "

"Mom's really bad at math," I tried lamely. "She—"

But Miss Thompson went right on. " 'I only have one child,' she kept repeating, just as though *I* were an idiot! Really! I know Jellimiah is a difficult boy, but that is no reason to deny his existence! I told your mother that. Then, I regret to say, she lost her temper entirely. I am just glad that *I* did not lose *my* temper with her as she did with me. It is hard to imagine, but she called me a lunatic. Me! A lunatic! I don't know what to do. I am considering calling in the authorities."

"I wouldn't do that," I pleaded. "Please don't. I think, um, it sounds like a miscommunication," I told her desperately, recalling what Mom had said. "That's it. A miscommunication."

"But your mother called me a lunatic and a madwoman!" cried Miss Thompson, starting to sound like she really was half crazed. "And some other things besides! She said I wasn't fit to work with young people. I heard her distinctly. She was shouting."

I thought quickly. (I'm getting pretty good at thinking quickly.)

"Um," I began, "my mom must have thought you were someone else. That's it. She thought you were someone else. In fact," I continued, "she must have thought you were our former neighbor in Los Angeles. Um, her name was Miss Thompson, too. It was! And she *hated* Jellimiah. Yes, she did. In fact, she always told our mom that as far as she was concerned, Mom had only one son. So I bet my mom thought it was *that* Miss Thompson, calling from California to annoy her. So when Mom said she has only one son, she was just kind of teasing the other Miss Thompson. And that's why she called you a lunatic and all that other stuff. You see, *that* Miss Thompson really was a lunatic. Really."

When I left the principal's office a bit later and headed for first-period study hall, I wasn't sure if I'd satisfied Miss Thompson. But I think I had. She was mumbling something to herself about how coincidental coincidences were.

I was so busy thinking about Miss Thompson that I almost didn't see Missy pass me in the hall. She was going to Latin, but she stopped to talk when she saw me. I held on tight to my notebook. I didn't want to do to Missy's toe what I'd done to Sondra's!

"Hi, John," she said, giving me a big smile. "Are you feeling better?"

"Better?" I asked.

"You were absent yesterday," Missy reminded me.

"Oh, that. Yes. Lots," I replied. "Um, Missy," I continued shyly, "do you feel like reading something I've written? I just finished it."

"Sure," said Missy. "Jellimiah says you're a good writer."

I handed her "The New Boy" and headed for study hall feeling pleased with myself. If that didn't impress Missy, then nothing would.

I was still feeling pleased with myself when I sat down in Mr. Fishwell's science class.

"Ah," he said, "you're back. I suppose your brother is absent, then?"

I nodded. "His ligament," I replied.

"Well, gang," Mr. Fishwell said to the class, "it's another good day."

"Why?" asked Cindi.

"Because the *right* twin is present."

I was fuming about this as I took out my book, and even now it still makes me mad. It isn't fair of Mr. Fishwell to criticize Jellimiah like that. I mean, Jellimiah hasn't done anything to him.

We were still learning about the skeletal system. But today was different. When I raised my hand to say something, Mr. Fishwell called on me immediately. Poor Cindi had her little hand in the air for ages, but Mr. Fishwell never seemed to turn his big head in her direction.

"Thank you, John," said Mr. Fishwell when I'd finished with a comment I'd been making. "That was most illuminating. I only wish your brother was as interested in sharing such well-thought-out contributions with the class."

I couldn't help it. I rose to my feet. I was trembling. I was scared. And I was mad. I hardly felt like me. I felt more like Jellimiah.

"I . . . I . . ." I began nervously.

"I can't hear you!" called Whip from the back of the room.

"I don't think that's a fair thing to say," I told Mr. Fishwell in a soft voice.

94

"I still can't hear you!" said Whip.

"I said you're not being fair, Mr. Fishwell," I said in a loud, clear Jellimiah voice. I couldn't believe it was me. I still can't!

"What did you say?" grunted Mr. Fishwell, glaring at me.

"It's not fair to make mean comments about my brother. Or any kid. You said Jellimiah wasn't interested in sharing, but how would you know? You never even call on him, just because you don't like the way he looks, or because of something you heard about his reputation. He's perfectly well behaved in science, but you don't give him a chance! You even act like he's a burglar. It's not fair!"

"Whoa!" said Jake. "Way to go!"

"Someone had to say it," said Cindi, breathing deeply but not hyperventilating.

Mr. Fishwell just stood there with his huge mouth hanging open. My mouth was open, too. He couldn't believe I had just said what I'd just said. I couldn't believe it, either. It was a Jellimiah thing to do—and I was John today.

But it felt good anyway. And I wasn't rude. I just told the truth.

"Of course I'd call on your brother, but he shows no interest in contributing," claimed Mr. Fishwell, getting red.

"He almost breaks his arm trying to get you to notice him," I said. "But you don't. Or, more exactly, you won't."

"How would you know?" demanded Mr. Fishwell. "It's not as though you and your brother have ever been here on the same day."

Albert, who was sitting next to me, let out a low chuckle.

"We're very close," I said. "Almost like one person. And I won't have you insulting me—I mean, insulting my brother. It's not like Jellimiah ever did anything really bad to you anyway, except to save the entire lab class from getting blown up. So leave my brother alone."

An explosion followed, and it wasn't a gas explosion. It was Mr. Fishwell and it was like a mini-volcano. His face turned molten red—and I almost expected to see hot lava come steaming out of his ears!

"Get your rude self to Miss Thompson's office!" he finally barked. "And tell her that she should suspend you *and* your brother. Get out! *Get out!*"

I felt like a balloon that's been suddenly deflated. I stumbled to the door, half mad and half embarrassed. I was thinking that being Jellimiah maybe wasn't such a hot idea after all.

I'd almost made it to the door when I heard a commotion behind me.

I looked back to see Cindi rising to her feet. She was trembling like a leaf, but she still managed to speak loud and clear.

"John is right," she gasped out. "You never call on me either, because my older sister didn't like science. I do, but you don't even give me a chance, just because Judie wasn't a science buff. It's not fair. It isn't."

Then Jake rose to his feet.

"Hey, man," he said. "Like, this is totally bogus. All John did was tell Mr. Fishwell to leave his brother alone. Whoa! If that's against the rules, then I say forget the rules! I'm going with John!"

"Me too!" gasped Cindi. "Jellimiah saved our lives, and all Mr. Fishwell does is pick on him. It's not nice!"

To my amazement, Jake and Cindi joined me by the door.

"Count me in, too," said Whip nervously. I knew he was worried about Mr. Fishwell giving him a low grade for walking out, but he walked out anyway. I admire that. Whip really *is* an okay guy. I was right about him after all.

"You four get back in here!" hollered Mr. Fishwell, forgetting he'd told me to get out.

I noticed Sondra looking around nervously. I saw her and Val conferring rapidly. Then they stood up together.

"My father's a lawyer," Sondra told Mr. Fishwell, "and he'll sue the pants off you if you don't stop hassling Jellimiah Jensen."

And Sondra and Val joined us by the door.

That did it—both for Mr. Fishwell and for the rest of the class.

Mr. Fishwell turned so red he looked like an enormous tomato that had been put in a microwave and was about to burst.

And once Sondra got up to go, the class followed. After all, she *is* the most popular girl at Edgewood Junior High.

It was another walkout, only this time it didn't have to do with a gas leak.

"Get back in here!" shouted the bright red Mr. Fishwell.

"No way!" Jake shouted back.

"What now?" gasped Cindi nervously, looking up and down the hallway.

"If only Jellimiah were here," cried Sondra. "*He'd* know what to do!"

I gulped.

"Well, I'm here," I said loudly. "And I say we—we . . ."

"See," interrupted Sondra. "John doesn't know what to do. *Jellimiah* would know what—"

But *I* interrupted *her*.

"C'mon," I shouted. "We're going to march on Miss Thompson's office. Let's go!"

Thursday, September 13, later at night

I had to stop for dinner. Now I can start again. I want to get everything down before I forget it. Here I go.

It was lunchtime, and I wasn't eating alone—me, John! Sondra and Val were with me. So were Jake, Whip, and Cindi. Albert Causley came over, too. They seemed pretty impressed.

It *was* impressive, if I say so myself. I can still hardly believe I did it!

We arrived at Miss Thompson's office and all of us just marched right past the secretary.

"What on earth is going on here?" cried Miss Thompson as we barged in.

So I told her.

"Nonsense, John," she began. "Mr. Fishwell is a respected teacher with many years' experience. He wouldn't—"

"But he did," said Cindi bravely.

"You didn't like it when you thought my mother was denying that Jellimiah existed," I told Miss Thompson. "Well, Mr. Fishwell's been doing the same thing. He won't even give Jellimiah a chance."

Miss Thompson looked a bit guilty. I guess she knew she'd done the same thing herself.

"But—" she began, when Jake interrupted.

"Like, whoa, Miss Thompson," he said. "He did."

"He did," echoed Sondra. "He said it was a good day because Jellimiah was absent. *I* think it's a *bad* day when Jellimiah's absent." And Sondra gave one of her sweet smiles.

Miss Thompson sighed and shook her head.

Then she spoke.

She was speaking to all of us, but I noticed she was looking at me.

"I shall have a talk with Mr. Fishwell," she said in a soft voice. "I am not saying I believe what you're telling me. But I am not saying I disbelieve it, either. I am saying that I shall look into it."

"Way cool, Miss T.," said Jake.

"It is almost your lunch period," continued Miss Thompson. "I shall not send you back to science. You may go to lunch early."

So we did.

It was like a party. And I was the guest of honor. Me, John! I was glad no one noticed I was trembling with delayed fear.

Even Sondra was nice to me.

"I'm so glad you stood up for Jellimiah," she told me.

"I'm glad you stood up for *all* of us," added Cindi. "Nobody has to be as mean as Mr. Fishwell is."

"Just wait till I tell my father," vowed Sondra. "He'll sue the pants off Mr. Fishwell."

Albert grinned and said nothing.

I started smiling, and the smile stayed on my face all the way through French and math. Even when Jellimiah's quiz came back with a B- on it, I was still smiling. I had the feeling that my story for our class literary magazine would change all *that*. Of course, now I wanted to change my story—I wanted to add a new part about "Mr. Sharkwell."

Maybe I could ask Missy for advice, I thought. She must have already read the story. Boy, she was really going to like me now, I decided. Maybe I'd stay John after all.

Of course, I mused as I headed for English, that meant tomorrow would have to be Jellimiah's last day. I wondered how I was going to get rid of him—and what I was going to do without him. I like him.

But now, I thought, who needed him? I was suddenly almost as popular as he was! And I hadn't even planned it—all I did was lose my temper, for about the first time in my life.

"Hi, Missy," I said as I walked into English class, still feeling pretty good. I started to sit down in the empty seat next to hers.

"I'm saving that seat for Nick," said Missy in a cold voice.

"What?" I said. "But I—"

"Here's your story back," said Missy in a frosty voice, almost throwing the paper at me. "I think you're the biggest jerk I've ever met."

"But—"

"I don't even want to talk to you," snapped Missy. "I'm too upset."

"But—" I tried again, but Missy just turned away from me.

"Liar," she said under her breath. "Creep. Bad writer.

Jerk," she added as Nick sat down next to her. He seemed to be glaring at me.

I wondered what I had done. Could Missy have found out I'm not really twins? I didn't think so.

It didn't make sense.

I brooded all the way through English. I kept trying to catch Missy's eye, but she avoided me.

After class I tried to talk with her in the hallway.

"Leave me alone!" she snapped. "Never talk to me again! You're a creep! I feel sorry for Jellimiah, having a twin brother like you!"

And she stormed off.

I was so busy trying to figure out why she suddenly hated me, I barely heard a *clip-clop, clip-clop* heading my way.

"John," came Miss Thompson's crisp voice, "I want you to know two things. I have, as promised, spoken with Mr. Fishwell, and I believe he will be more, ah, cooperative from now on. We shall overlook your leading a walkout this morning, provided nothing like it reoccurs. However, I am concerned about your attitude. It seems to be changing."

"But—"

"So," interrupted Miss Thompson, "it made me interested in knowing more about you and your brother."

Uh-oh, I thought. "We're not all *that* interesting," I said.

"At any rate," continued Miss Thompson, "after an hour on the phone, I was at last able to locate someone in Los Angeles who could provide me with your complete records. It was apparently a bad connection, or else a stupid individual, because each time I said I wanted both records, she said there was only one. At least that's what it sounded like."

"When will they come?" I asked with a sinking heart.

"They are being faxed to me sometime this afternoon. Alas, I have a meeting with the school board," sighed Miss Thompson. "Sad to say, they seem to think these burglaries are my fault! If only I hadn't opened that closet door when Jellimiah captured the burglar! Oh, well. I won't be here to received the records, but I shall read the fax first thing tomorrow morning. I just wanted you to know. That is all. Now I'm off to my meeting."

And Miss Thompson trotted down the hallway on her giraffe legs.

First Missy, now this! It's like the end of the world. I guess I can always run away, or convince my Mom to send me to a private school after all.

But no.

I've come too far to turn back now. I'm really starting to like Edgewood Junior High. And kids are even starting to like me. Me, John. Not just Jellimiah. Well, I have to admit it—they like both of us. And I like them, too. I like Whip and Jake and Cindi and Albert. I'm not so sure I like Sondra, but I still have a crush on her anyway. And I sure like Missy, even if she hates me all of a sudden.

Maybe I can't change Missy's mind—much less figure it out—but maybe I can do something about those records.

But what?

I have an idea what Jellimiah would do.

Should *I* do it?

Do I have a choice?

Friday, September 14, 1:30 A.M.

As I set off around midnight, I wished I really did have a twin. It would have been great to have Jellimiah with me. But in a way he *was* with me. I mean, I *am* Jellimiah—at least part of me is. I'm not just plain old me anymore, plain John Jensen. Yesterday changed all that.

When I led that walkout, I did something plain old John Jensen never ever could have done. And as I headed toward the school tonight, I realized I was doing something else he never would have done. Maybe I'm more like my grandfather than I realized.

At any rate, as I trudged down Edgewood Avenue I certainly hoped I was. I was going to need to be pretty brave to do what I was planning to do.

No, not pretty brave—*very* brave.

Edgewood Junior High stood lost in darkness as I rounded the last turn in its long drive and surveyed it from behind a tree. I clutched my flashlight to my chest. It was an old one from when I went to sleepaway camp the summer after third grade. It even has "JELLIMIAH" written on it in big capital letters. I hoped I wouldn't drop it the way I've been dropping my notebook lately. What if I dropped it and it broke and I couldn't find my way out?

I tried to think of other things.

Like Missy.

She really doesn't seem to like me anymore.

So I thought of Sondra.

I'm not so sure I like her anymore.

So I started thinking of who I should become, John or Jellimiah. Jellimiah or John?

I drew closer and closer to the main building.

Then something grabbed my shoulder.

I screamed, tripped, and dropped my flashlight. "Don't shoot!" I cried.

Silence.

I looked up from where I'd fallen.

There was no one there.

I was sure I'd felt someone grabbing my shoulder, though.

Looking up I saw a low-hanging branch shaking violently.

So *that* was what had grabbed me!

I crawled around on all fours until I found my flashlight. I was lucky—it still worked.

I took a deep breath and tiptoed right up to the building.

Before I left school yesterday, I sneaked into the office and left a window slightly ajar. But just slightly, so no one would notice.

"Please still be open, please still be open!" I prayed in a whisper as I edged up to the window.

I took another deep breath and reached up for the window. I found it. I gave a quick pull. Nothing. I pulled harder. Yes! It was still open.

I opened it wide and peeked through. The office was black and empty.

The coast was clear.

With my heart in my throat I pulled myself up and crawled through.

I was there! I had done it! I was in the front office of Edgewood Junior High at twelve-thirty in the morning!

Me, John Jensen!

Okay, maybe I was trembling a bit. Okay, maybe like a leaf. But I still was there. Alone.

I took some more deep breaths and pretended I wasn't scared.

Now, I told myself, *all you have to do is grab those faxes and run for it before the night watchman shows up.* I hoped he wasn't armed. I didn't feel like getting shot.

I listened.

Silence. Total silence.

I switched on my flashlight and began searching.

I found the fax machine—but no records. Maybe they hadn't arrived.

But maybe they had. Then where would they be?

I turned off the flashlight and felt my way to Miss Thompson's office. I'd been there often enough to know the way almost by heart: through the front office, into a little hallway, past a bathroom and the small room containing the copy machine, and then into Miss Thompson's office.

Once I was in her office, I switched my flashlight back on. I knew the less I used it, the less chance I had of being spotted.

I shone it on her desk.

There was a letter from Ms. Nolan, president of the school board.

I glanced at it.

Poor Miss Thompson! I read only the first paragraph—I'm not completely nosy!—but it said they held her responsible for all the burglaries and unless she gets busy and stops them, they're going to consider replacing her. No wonder she quivers and throbs so much!

But there were no faxes on her desk.

Then I remembered about in and out boxes.

But did Miss Thompson have them?

Sure enough, there they were, on top of a file cabinet, in the corner of the office.

I went through the papers in the in box.

No . . . no . . . no . . . no . . . wait a minute—what was that?

"Official Records: City of Los Angeles, California," it began.

I had found it. And I had come prepared.

I replaced the records with a one-page fax I'd faxed to myself that afternoon. "Jensen records lost," it read.

I doubt Miss Thompson will give up easily, but at least I have her stalled. And once there's only one of us, maybe she'll care less about us.

I sure hope so.

I crammed the faxes into the inner pocket of my jacket and headed out of Miss Thompson's office, back toward the open window in the front office. I had to leave that way—the land sloped away, which meant Miss Thompson's office was on the second floor. I didn't feel like falling and spraining my ligament or hurting my wrist for real!

I was at the door to the little hallway when my heart

stopped beating. I heard footsteps, and it wasn't my imagination. They were coming my way!

I thought I was going to throw up. I got so nervous I
couldn't find the switch to turn off the flashlight.

Luckily, that didn't matter—I dropped the stupid thing
and it switched off all by itself as it rolled back into Miss
Thompson's office.

I darted back into the office, kicking my flashlight across
the floor as I did. I was getting pretty sick of that place! I
practically threw myself under Miss Thompson's desk, hit-
ting my head on the edge.

My teeth were chattering, my head hurt, and I was shaking from fear. I was thinking that I never should have imagined that I, John Jensen, could get away with this. Maybe
Jellimiah could. But not me. No way.

Trying to stop my teeth from chattering, I listened to the
footsteps. Maybe whoever it was would just walk on by.

But instead the footsteps got louder and louder, closer
and closer.

They were coming right toward Miss Thompson's office!

What if it was Miss Thompson, burning the midnight oil?

No, they didn't clip-clop. So it wasn't Miss Thompson.

It was a heavy tread. And it sounded like more than one
person. But I knew there was only one night watchman. I
was sure I heard two people. For a moment I thought
maybe I was just hearing the mad beating of my heart.

Then the footsteps entered Miss Thompson's office, and
I heard voices—two of them.

It hadn't been my heart.

"Well, Gus," said one, flipping on the light, "let's sit for
a minute."

"Fine by me," said Gus. "This is the most comfortable
room in the entire school."

Next I heard them sitting down in the two easy chairs right next to Miss Thompson's desk, the chairs where she and I have had a few too many conversations.

"What did we get tonight, Mickey?" asked Gus.

"Some more VCRs, three CD players, and some electronic equipment. We should clear some decent money."

Gus chuckled. "Man," he said, "this gig of yours as a night watchman sure has paid off!"

"You said it," agreed Mickey. "And no one suspects me. After all, my record is as clean as new-fallen snow—not even one parking ticket!"

"I wish I could say the same for mine," said Gus. "But who cares? They can't trace me to you. And no one knows you slipped me those extra master keys you made. I think we've just about cleaned this place out, don't you, Mickey?"

"Yup. We've done good."

"Except for the time that kid locked me in the closet," mused Gus. "Man, was I lucky that principal is half crazy or something. She just let me walk on out of here!"

"Served you right for pulling a burglary during the day," said Mickey.

"It worked before," chuckled Gus. "Remember, that idiot kid even helped me load the computers into my van! What a prize jerk!"

No one was going to call me a prize jerk and get away with it! All of a sudden I stopped being scared out of my mind and started getting angry. I had to get revenge. I had to. But how?

I thought. And I thought some more.

Nothing.

Then I pretended I was Jellimiah. What would he do? Instantly an idea popped into my head. It might not work . . . but then it might. I'd have to be careful. Really careful. Not to mention very lucky.

Slowly, quietly, I took a pencil out of my pocket. Then, slowly, quietly, I reached up above my head, up to Miss Thompson's desktop. Gus and Mickey were still so busy chatting, I felt pretty confident they wouldn't notice.

My hand reached around. I felt a schedule book . . . a pen . . . a glass with something that sloshed around in it as I nudged it. Finally my hand touched a notepad. Cautiously I slid it off the desktop and brought it down to my lap.

Perfect! At the top was printed "From the Desk of Judith Thompson."

In an adult-style handwriting I wrote something on Miss Thompson's stationery. Then, just as carefully, I replaced the notepad on top of the desk.

But how to make Gus and Mickey notice what I'd written?

I didn't have time to think that one through, though, since at that moment they got up to go. It was now or never!

I could hear Mickey rising from his chair with a grunt.

"These late hours are getting to me," he complained.

He took a step sideways, away from the chair. I was pretty sure he'd have his back to Miss Thompson's desk even though I could tell from his breathing that he was standing right next to it now.

As quick as a cat pouncing, I reached up and toppled the half-filled glass that was on top of the desk.

"Darn it!" growled Mickey. "I musta knocked up against the desk. Look what I did. There's water everywhere!"

Gus came over to look—and luckily they were both standing on the far side of the desk, so they couldn't see me underneath.

"Never mind the water," said Gus in an excited voice. "Look at this note that dumb lady left lying on the desk!"

"Let me see," said Mickey, picking up the note I had just left. " 'Ten thousand in cash hidden in the copy room. Remember to bring to bank on Friday,' " he read aloud.

"Tomorrow's Friday," said Gus. "So that means the dough is still there."

"What are we waiting for?" asked Mickey, and the two men hightailed it out of Miss Thompson's office. A second later I heard the sound of excited searching going on in the copy room.

"It's gotta be in here somewhere!" I heard Gus telling Mickey.

Dream on, I said to myself, tiptoeing closer and closer to the copy room.

I slammed the door shut and, before Gus and Mickey could react, I bolted it shut from the outside. Their master keys were no use against a dead bolt.

"Let us outta here!" they hollered. They were pounding on the door and kicking it, too. But it was a good strong door. I knew it wouldn't budge. And I knew it was a decent-sized room, so they wouldn't suffocate.

I taped a note to the front door of the office, so Miss Thompson would see it on the way in. Here's what I wrote:

Dear Miss T.,

There's a surprise waiting for you in the copy room. Don't open the door this time! Call the police before you do anything! This should end those burglaries once and for all!

Signed,
A Friend

Then, before I left, I stopped once more in front of the door to the copy room.

"Hey, you in there!" I called loudly. "Remember this: I am *not* a prize jerk!"

Friday, September 14, after school

"John," Mom was saying over breakfast this morning, "you look tired. Are you feeling all right?"

"I'm fine, Mom," I said, trying not to yawn. I didn't get home until one-thirty last night, and I was too excited to fall asleep right away, so I wrote in this journal for at least an hour. I sure had a lot to write about!

I still can't believe I did it. But I did. Me, John Jensen!

Mom sipped her coffee. I could tell she had something on her mind again.

"John," Mom finally said, "I got a strange message at the hospital yesterday from your Miss Thompson."

"She is not *my* Miss Thompson," I protested, even though I probably had just saved her job for her.

But Mom paid no attention. "What she said made no sense whatsoever. None."

"What did she say?" I asked with a sinking feeling.

"The message said that she wanted me to know she was not from California, in case I was confused about it." Mom snorted. "I think *she's* the confused one around here! I have half a mind to report her to the school board!"

"I wouldn't do that, Mom," I said, and quickly told Mom about all the trouble Miss Thompson was in because of the burglaries. "I bet it's just the stress," I concluded.

"Well," said Mom, "let's hope someone catches the burglars before she goes completely around the bend!"

"I think there's a pretty good chance of that," I said with a smile.

Mom just shook her head.

Five minutes after she left for the hospital, I was Jellimiah. With moussed hair and completely ripped clothes that the breeze blew through, I stomped off to school.

John or Jellimiah? Jellimiah or John? The choice loomed ahead of me. It was going to be somebody's last day— but whose?

The sound of sirens interrupted my thinking. Three police cars were whizzing down the drive from Edgewood Junior High. I looked quickly and saw that one had two men in the backseat. They sure didn't look happy!

I grinned. This time Miss Thompson *had* waited for the police to arrive before she opened the door.

"Jellimiah!" shrieked Miss Thompson as I stomped by the front office. "Where is your brother? I have the most wonderful news!"

"He has a headache," I replied. "Too much studying, I guess."

"Oh, dear," said Miss Thompson, "sick again! And I so wanted him to be the first to know."

"Well," I said, "you can tell me and I'll tell him as soon as I can."

So Miss Thompson told me.

"Really!" I said. "Locked in the copy room and no one knows how! And a mysterious note attached to the office door! How amazing!"

"Isn't it!" cried Miss Thompson, beaming from ear to ear. She was so thrilled that her nostrils forgot to quiver and her veins forgot to bulge. She looked almost human.

Soon the news spread all over school—the burglars had been caught. Some of the kids had heard that Miss Thompson had caught them single-handed and wrestled them to the floor! Val had heard that *I* was one of the thieves!

Missy still seemed mad at me—I mean, at John. When I walked into English she shot me a pitying look. I sat down next to her and said, "Hey, my brother tells me you're sort of mad at him."

"Not just sort of," snapped back Missy. "Very. And you can tell him from me that until he confesses, I for one will never talk to him again. Never."

"But what did he do?"

"I'm no tattletale," said Missy. "If your own twin hasn't told you, then I certainly am not going to, even though it involves you." And she would say no more.

Mr. Forester had something to say, too, but he also wouldn't say it to me.

"It's about John's story for the literary magazine," Mr. Forester told me, which kind of mystified me. I mean, I hadn't even handed it in. Only Missy had seen it. I wondered if she had shown it to Mr. Forester, and whether her being mad could have something to do with the story.

"We'll be printing our first issue shortly," Mr. Forester continued, "and I wanted to speak with John as soon as possible. Any chance your brother will be in school later on?"

The chances suddenly got pretty good.

"He might be here after study hall," I said, thinking ahead.

I decided I had to get John to school—I wanted to know why Missy was so angry with me, and I wanted to get my story in the first issue. If I ended up being John, I wanted to be known as a hard-hitting journalist. That had to impress Missy. It had to!

"Fine," said Mr. Forester. "Make sure John comes and talks to me," he added. I noticed he had an odd expression on his face.

And I noticed someone else had an odd expression. Albert had been listening to my conversation with Mr. Forester, and when I said that John would be in after study hall, he almost fell off his chair. What a weirdo!

Mr. Fishwell was absent today, which only made it easier for me to carry out my plan. I guess he's just getting his head together before he faces John Jensen again. Maybe he'll never come back!

The entire Science Class was sent to Study Hall. Only Sondra was missing.

"She's home getting ready for the party," Val whispered to me. "She can't wait! And everybody seems so happy about it this year! Sondra told me even the nerds seemed delighted. They all kept running up to her yesterday and saying, 'See you at the party,' 'See you at the party,' until Sondra thought she would, like, barf or something! But I guess that means the nerds didn't notice they were all going to the same nerd party next week! We pulled it off! Isn't that neat?"

"Very neat," I said.

Mr. Fishwell's absence gave me two study halls in a row. That gave me plenty of time.

I slipped out a side door and made my way home.

At home I changed into John's clothes and slicked down my hair. Just in case I wanted to become Jellimiah again, I brought some mousse and his raggedy clothes along with me in my backpack. The boots didn't fit in the pack, so I left them behind. I mean, once in a while Jellimiah could be seen wearing regular shoes.

"John!" exclaimed Mr. Forester. "You're here!"

"I had a headache," I said, "but I started to feel better, so I came to school. Jellimiah said you wanted to see me."

"It's about your story, 'The New Boy,'" began Mr. Forester.

"I didn't even hand it in yet," I said, feeling confused.

Mr. Forester looked a bit confused, too. "Oh," he finally said, "I see. You printed it out, right?"

I nodded.

"Well, when you printed out a copy for yourself, Nick's system automatically saved it. Later, Nick and I printed out a second copy of everything that the system had saved that way. I guess I assumed you wanted to submit it. Do you?"

"You bet."

"Good," said Mr. Forester, "because it's good—really good. But there are two things I want to talk to you about. First, this story is going to make waves. Now, I don't believe in censorship, but before it's printed, I just wanted to make sure you know what you might be in for. There are some folks who won't be too pleased."

I thought of Mr. Trotter. He'll be lucky if all that happens is he gets written about in a story under a fake name. He'll have time to change his ways before he really gets in trouble. And besides, he was mean to me when I was John. And then there was Mr. Fishwell. Well, I only told the truth.

And he'd made Cindi cry. And I hadn't even added that part about the walkout.

But then I thought of Whip, and I felt bad. I decided I should talk to him before I agreed to have my story printed.

"There *is* one person I'd like to talk to," I told Mr. Forester. "Let me get back to you after I do."

Mr. Forester nodded. "Then there's the second thing I want to mention to you, something a certain student spoke to me about."

"Yes?" I said, feeling nervous and holding on tighter to my notebook.

"Well John—" began Mr. Forester, but then the bell rang. He looked at his watch. "I've got a class coming in," he told me, "and this is something I'd rather discuss in private. We'll finish this later."

I went off in search of Whip, wondering what Mr. Forester could have been told and who it was that had told him. I guessed it was Missy.

I found Whip on his way to Spanish.

"Sure," he said. "Señora Gonzales can wait. What's up?"

I blushed. This wasn't going to be easy.

"It's about math," I began. "It's about those quizzes."

Whip blushed, too. His thick neck turned a bright red.

"I wrote a story about being new here," I went on, picking my words carefully, "and I wrote about how a certain math teacher gives good grades to his football players, grades they don't deserve."

"Right on," said Whip. "I hate it when he does that. It makes people think all football players are dumb. And we're not."

I stared at Whip. I couldn't understand why he was saying this. Every time I'd seen him write down the answer to a question, it was wrong!

117

"But . . . but . . ." I stammered.

"Yeah," said Whip in a soft voice, "I know why you're hesitating."

"You do?"

"Yeah," continued Whip. "It's on account of Jellimiah."

"Jellimiah?" I wasn't following any of this.

"Like, I know he's an ace football player and all, but he can't do math worth beans. He's been trying to copy from me every time we have a quiz! I hate that! So I did what I always do when I know someone's copying me—I write down the wrong answer on purpose. Then I go back later and put in the right one."

"You mean you can do math after all?" I gasped.

"It's not my best subject," admitted Whip, "but I usually get at least a B-minus average."

"Wow!" I said. "That's great!"

Whip shrugged. "It's all right," he said. "Listen, I've gotta get to Spanish sooner or later. Thanks for talking to me. You're an okay guy, you know, even if you don't play football or anything. And tell Jellimiah I won't rat on him, but he really has to stop trying to cheat."

And with that Whip trotted off before I could explain that Jellimiah hadn't been cheating. I decided I'd explain the whole thing to him later.

But at least I'd made a friend—sort of. I didn't know Whip was so cool. And he likes me—John, that is.

It just makes it that much harder to decide whether I should stay John or become Jellimiah.

I was thinking so hard I didn't look where I was going. I knocked right into Albert. He was standing in the hall, drawing a picture.

He stared at me as though he'd seen a ghost.

"I'm sorry I ran into you," I said.

"I don't believe it. I don't believe it," he kept repeating.

Leaving Albert not to believe whatever he wasn't believing, I raced off to find Mr. Forester.

I passed Missy in the hall. She positively glared at me.

"Missy," I said, stopping to talk, "could you please—"

"John Jensen," interrupted Missy, "I never want to speak with you again as long as I live."

"But—"

"As long as I live," she said again. Then she turned her back on me and stalked off down the hall.

Maybe I should stay Jellimiah, I thought. At least Missy isn't mad at *him!*

"John!" came an ear-piercing shriek from behind me. "You're here after all!" Then came the all-too familiar *clip-clop, clip-clop.* I was cornered.

"Have you heard?" gushed Miss Thompson. "I so wanted you to be the first to know!"

"I was," I said with a smile.

"But you weren't," said Miss Thompson. "I had to tell Jellimiah before I told you. But at least I'm glad he let you know! Isn't it just too wonderful? And how in the world they managed to lock themselves in I shall never know. Never! Perhaps the bolt just slid to the locked position when they shut the door! But why they should want to tear apart the copy room I shall never understand! Never! And who on earth could have left me that note? I am beside myself with joy!"

And with that, Miss Thompson gave me a big kiss.

Yuck!

And to make it worse, Jake saw her do it!

Now I'd have to stay Jellimiah! What if Jake told everyone that I'd been seen kissing Miss Thompson? Forget it! I'd be ruined!

"My job is saved! Saved!" Miss Thompson shrieked and ran off madly down the hall.

"She made me do it," I said weakly to Jake, who was snickering by some lockers.

"Aw, don't worry man," he said. "She even kissed *me* one time! And besides, you're Jellimiah's twin bro. And you led that walkout on Mr. Fishface. You're all right in my book."

And Jake slapped me hard on the back before he stomped off in his Jellimiah boots.

Thinking that maybe I'd stay John after all, I headed toward Mr. Forester's room. I was almost there when I saw Sondra. Van had told me she was staying home today. What was she doing in school?

"Uh, John," she said, giving me one of her famous smiles, "is Jellimiah around? I have *got* to talk to him."

"He's in the bathroom," I said, pointing behind me. "I'll go get him. It'll take just a second. You wait here."

I darted into the bathroom. Out of the backpack came the mousse and the ripped clothes; into it went my John clothes.

"Hey, Sondra," I said, leaving the bathroom, "like, what are you doing here?"

"Oh, Jellimiah," cooed Sondra, "I was wondering if you'd help Val and me do some last-minute shopping after school. Can you come, too?"

"Sure," I said. "Why not? But you came all the way to school to ask me. Why didn't you call me last night?"

"How could I?" asked Sondra, shaking her pretty head. "I tried, but your number's unlisted."

No wonder no one ever calls me! I forgot no one has my number!

"It's because my mom's a doctor," I explained. "If a doctor has a listed number, their patients are always calling them at home."

"Same for lawyers," said Sondra. "We have an unlisted number, too. Anyway, I gotta run before someone sees me. I'm supposed to be home sick! See you at three. My mom will pick up you and Val. Bye-bye!"

Off ran Sondra. I ran off, too. Back into the bathroom. Back to being John. I had to dunk my head in the sink to get the mousse out. I did my best to dry it with paper towels, but it was still pretty damp. Then I whipped off my Jellimiah clothes and got back into my John clothes. Phew! It's a good thing I'm a speedy dresser.

"I'm John, I'm John," I reminded myself just before I pushed open the door to Mr. Forester's room.

"It's okay about the story," I told him as I entered.

"Fine," he said. "It's going to make people sit up and notice our first issue. Now," he continued, "about that other thing."

I sat down in the empty classroom.

Mr. Forester cleared his throat and began.

"John," he said, "this makes me feel very uncomfortable, but, well, another student has reported that it was your brother, not you, who actually wrote this story."

"What?"

"You see," continued Mr. Forester, "it's dated Wednesday, September twelfth—and you were absent that day, John. It was Jellimiah who was here that day."

I gulped. I turned white. I turned red. I knew this was making me look guilty. I just couldn't help it. At last I write something decent, and no one believes I wrote it!

"John," said Mr. Forester gently, "is there something you'd like to tell me?"

"Well," I said, stalling for time, "it's like this . . ."

"Yes?" said Mr. Forester.

I thought, and thought quickly, too.

"I wrote it at home," I said, "and I gave Jellimiah my handwritten draft to put into the computer since I was absent that day. We help each other out that way. 'Cause we're twins and all."

"Hmm," said Mr. Forester, "I see. That makes sense. But there's something else, John." And here Mr. Forester produced that stupid story I'd written, "Moveing." "This was saved automatically, too, and it's dated the eleventh—when you were here and Jellimiah was absent. Did you write this?"

"Oh, that!" I said. "That was a joke! Really. Sometimes Jellimiah and I, um, we kind of amuse ourselves by writing the dumbest thing we can think of. It wasn't a real story or anything."

"I guess it *is* too bad to be real," said Mr. Forester. "I'm glad that's almost cleared up."

"Me too," I said. "What do you mean, *almost?*"

"I mean I'd like to hear the same thing from Jellimiah before I sign off on your story."

"You want to see Jellimiah?" I asked.

"That's the general idea," replied Mr. Forester.

I sighed.

"I'll go get him," I said. "Wait here."

I tore out of the classroom, practically knocking over Albert, who was waiting outside for his turn to meet with Mr. Forester.

Three minutes later Jellimiah made his way out of the nearest bathroom into Mr. Forester's classroom. It's easier to become Jellimiah than it is to become John—the mousse is quicker to put in than it is to take out.

"Jellimiah," said Mr. Forester, "have a seat. Did your brother tell you what I wished to speak with you about?"

"Yes," I replied. "John told me all about it. Yes, John did write the story, and yes, I was just typing it for him from his handwritten draft. And yes, that other little story was only a joke."

Mr. Forester looked relieved.

"I am glad to hear it," he said. "I am also glad to hear you say 'Yes' instead of 'Yeah'. It sounds better."

"Wow, man," I said, "like I didn't mean to."

"It's all right to speak more like your brother," said Mr. Forester. "There's nothing wrong with proper grammar."

"Yeah man," I said, getting up to go.

On the way out I passed Albert again. This time I noticed he was carrying a portfolio—I guessed it held drawings he wanted to have included in the literary magazine.

"Hey, Jensen," he said, "maybe sometime you could write a story to go with my drawings."

"I'm not too good at making up stories," I said modestly.

"You?" said Albert. He almost dropped his portfolio, he started laughing so hard.

Suddenly I realized Albert was right. I *am* good at making things up—that's all I've been doing since school began!

When Albert calmed down, he gave me a look and said, "Nice shoes, Jensen."

"Thanks, man," I replied, wondering why Albert should notice my shoes.

"I saw your brother was wearing the exact same style," commented Albert.

"So?" I said. "We go shopping together."

Albert opened his eyes wide. "And you both spilled white paint on precisely the same spot?"

I looked down in a panic. I hadn't known there was paint on my shoes. That could give me away.

But there wasn't any paint.

I looked up at Albert.

He looked back at me.

"I'm a twin, remember," he said. "I know all about twins."

And with that he left me standing by the door.

Three minutes later, still wondering how much Albert knew, I was sitting in Mr. Trotter's math class.

Of course he was thrilled to see me, since I was Jellimiah. I sat there thinking he won't be thrilled about anything much once my story appears. It also hit me what a fool I've been—I should have said we *both* wrote it! Then, no matter who I decide to be, I'd get credit for it.

I was so busy thinking, I barely heard Mr. Trotter talking. Then I realized he was talking to me.

". . . how about it?" he was asking me expectantly.

"How about what?" I asked.

"How about joining us at practice today?" he said.

"Oh, you want my brother," I said. "He's the football star of the family."

"John plays football?" asked Mr. Trotter incredulously.

"No," I said, "Jellimiah plays football. He's the one you want to join you."

Mr. Trotter stared at me.

"But *you're* Jellimiah," he said.

"I am?" I said. I'd been so busy thinking, I'd forgotten who I was pretending to be. "I am?" I repeated. "I mean, um, I *am*. Yes. I am. Of course."

"Then," persisted Mr. Trotter, "will you join us for practice today?"

"My ligament," I said, pointing at my leg. "It's still twisted. Sprained. Whatever."

"Well, join us anyway," said Mr. Trotter. "You can referee."

"I'll see," I said. I had to get out of that! Mosquitoes know more about football than I do! I couldn't referee in a million years! "I might, um, have to take my brother to the doctor. He's got a terrible headache."

"Speaking of your brother," said Mr. Trotter, "where is he? Shouldn't he be in class?"

"I think he's, um, in the bathroom," I said. "He's not feeling well. I'd better go check on him."

"Don't forget you said you'd referee after school!" called Mr. Trotter as I raced from the room.

"Right," I said. They'd never find Jellimiah after school—I'd just change back into John.

Speaking of finding, there is someone *I* have to find at the party tonight: Missy. Now that I know why she's so mad at me, I have to explain that it's all a mistake. That I'm no plagiarist. I just want her to like me again, even if it is just as a friend. (I also wish Nick would move to Brazil and leave us alone.)

If Missy would stop being mad at me, I'd stay John forever and ever.

I decided not to go back to math class. Let them think I was with my sick brother in the bathroom.

I passed Cindi. She gave me a big smile.

"You and your brother are all right," she told me. "You've shaken up Edgewood like nobody else ever did. Even Mr. Fishwell! Maybe you'll find a way to make Sondra less snobby, too! And," she continued, "Nick showed me John's story. It was great."

"I'll tell him you said so."

Hmm. Cindi likes both John *and* Jellimiah.

John or Jellimiah . . . Jellimiah or John . . .

I'd just begun to head for the bathroom to change back into John—after all, I didn't want Whip or Mr. Trotter to see me as Jellimiah and drag me off to referee the football practice—when I felt sharp fingernails digging into my shoulder.

I wheeled around and saw Miss Thompson.

That was bad enough.

But what was dangling from the long fingers of her right hand was worse.

It was my flashlight—the one with my name written on it. I'd dropped it in her office.

I'd never get out of this one.

Never.

∽

Friday, September 14, after school—continued

Boy, just the memory of the expression on Miss Thompson's face was so horrible, I had to go have a snack. Now I'm back. Here's what happened next.

Miss Thompson led me into her office. I'd been hoping I'd never have to go back *there* again.

We sat down in the two chairs.

At least I didn't have to sit under the desk!

Miss Thompson waved the flashlight in front of my nose.

"Start talking, Jellimiah," she said. "And talk fast."

"About what?" I said. "It's not against the law to own a flashlight."

"I found it here in my office," said Miss Thompson in a cold voice. I noticed her nostrils were starting to quiver.

"So?" I said. "So what?"

"So," said Miss Thompson, "what was it doing here? The burglars were in my office—and so was your flashlight."

"Those burglars, they must have stolen the flashlight from my locker!" I cried. "I was wondering where it had gone! It was missing this morning!"

"Jellimiah," said Miss Thompson, "were you involved in these burglaries?"

"Me?" I cried. "No way! I helped capture the—"

I stopped.

I wished I could unsay what I'd just said.

"So it was you who locked them in the copy room," said Miss Thompson thoughtfully. "I couldn't imagine how that bolt slid shut all on its own."

I looked down at my lap.

I was sure I was going to get suspended. You aren't supposed to be hanging around the principal's office in the middle of the night.

All of a sudden I decided I didn't care if I got suspended. That would just make my decision easier. If Jellimiah got suspended, then I'd stay John.

It wouldn't be so bad being John now that I was better at it.

But I'd sure miss being Jellimiah.

"What, might I ask, were you doing in my office capturing burglars?" demanded Miss Thompson.

"It was John's idea," I blurted out.

"The dear boy," interrupted Miss Thompson.

It's so weird, how just the thought of John calms her down.

"Anyway," I said, "John heard the night watchman saying something suspicious, so we decided to investigate."

"But," interrupted Miss Thompson again, "when did John cross paths with him? The night watchman is never at school during the day."

"He isn't? I mean, of course not—he isn't. John was, um,

shopping. That's it. At the mall. And he overheard the night watchman there."

"But how did John recognize him?" Miss Thompson wanted to know.

"How did he recognize him?" My brain worked furiously, but I couldn't think of an answer to that one. Finally I gave up and said, "Um, John's full of surprises."

"The dear boy," repeated Miss Thompson. "But he took a dreadful risk, coming here alone at night."

"I was with him," I said.

Miss Thompson beamed at me.

"Perhaps I have misjudged you, just as Mr. Fishwell did," she said. And then she shook my hand.

It was strange to have her treating me like a human being all of a sudden, but I figure it's a good thing. If I stay Jellimiah, then Miss Thompson won't be bugging me all the time.

"One more thing," added Miss Thompson. "I received a fax from your former school. It's so disappointing—but your records have been lost."

"These things happen," I said calmly, but inside I was congratulating myself. She'd fallen for it!

"It hardly seems to matter now," said Miss Thompson in a friendly voice. "I'm sure you and I shall get along just fine now. And John is a lamb. Doubtless he was acting up a bit because he was upset that I'd misjudged his twin brother."

"Doubtless," I said. "Oh, and speaking of John, I'd better go and see how he is. His head is hurting him."

"The poor child," said Miss Thompson. "It's surely a result of last night's excitement. Just think of the danger you and he went through on my behalf! Why, you deserve a medal."

"Let's keep it our little secret," I said.

"But imagine," cried Miss Thompson, "an awards ceremony—you *and* John on the podium, receiving medals!"

"Impossible," I said flatly.

"Why would that be impossible?"

You'll never know, I thought. Out loud I said, "Because John is very shy about receiving awards. He hates them. He'd never accept one. Never."

"But I heard he won all sorts of awards in California," argued Miss Thompson.

"Oh, them," I said. I was beginning to lose track of what I'd said, and to whom. "Yeah, he *won* them, but he refused to go receive them. You know John."

"The dear boy," said Miss Thompson for the zillionth time. "The dear, dear boy."

"So," I said, "it'll be our little secret. Okay?"

"If that's what John would want, it's what I want, too. However," continued Miss Thompson, "promise me that neither you or your brother will ever, ever do anything so foolhardy again."

"I promise," I said. "And promise me you'll forget about an awards ceremony."

"I promise," said Miss Thompson.

Let's hope she keeps her promise for once!

I left Miss Thompson's office as the bell sounded three o'clock.

Part of me felt thrilled. And part of me felt sad.

Thrilled because I've gotten away with it. I've been twins for a week and a half and no one suspects. Well, maybe Albert has a clue.

And sad because today was either John's or Jellimiah's last day at Edgewood Junior High.

One of us has to go.

I was looking for Val when I saw Whip coming.

He couldn't see me! He might drag me off to referee! Then they'd know I was a phony!

I made a mad dash for the bathroom. I had just changed clothes and was washing the mousse out of my hair when the bathroom door opened.

"Hey, John," said Whip, "do you always wash your hair in school?"

"Um, no," I said, embarrassed. "But Miss Thompson spilled some, um, perfume on it and it stank. So I was just washing it out. That's it. Perfume."

"Yeah," agreed Whip from inside one of the stalls, "her perfume could stink up Yankee Stadium." He came out and washed his hands. "Where's Jellimiah?" he asked before he left. "We were hoping he'd ref for us at practice."

"Um, Jellimiah had to take me to the doctor," I said. It didn't come out the way I meant it to. I guess a day of lying was finally getting to me.

"Uh, if he's taking you to the doctor," asked Whip, "how come you're still here?"

"Because, um, he's, um . . . he's getting my books for me from my locker," I said.

Whip grinned. "It must be neat having a twin. I wish I had one."

"So do I," I said by mistake, but Whip didn't seem to hear. He'd already left the bathroom.

I stepped out of the boys' room—and practically knocked over Val.

"John," she said, "where's Jellimiah? I'm supposed to meet him here at three o'clock. Sondra's mother is picking us up."

"He's in the—" I began, then stopped.

I'd just seen Whip standing a ways down the hall. He

looked like he was waiting for someone. It wouldn't do for him to see Jellimiah leave the bathroom when he was supposed to be getting my books. And besides, how could Jellimiah leave the bathroom if he'd never gone in there in the first place?

I couldn't change into Jellimiah. I had to stay John.

"Uh, sorry, Val," I said, "but Jellimiah had to go home after school. It's an emergency. Our dog's sick."

"Gosh," said Val. "That's terrible."

It *was* terrible. Now I couldn't warn Sondra about what I'd done. She'll hate me for sure.

"There's Sondra's mom!" cried Val, heading for the door. "Tell Jellimiah to come to the party a bit early, okay?"

"Okay," I called. "And tell Sondra I'm sorry I couldn't come shopping."

"But you weren't invited," said Val from the door. "It was your brother. Remember?"

"Oh, that," I said hurriedly. "Sorry. I'm just so tired I can't remember who I am anymore."

"Having a sick dog will do that to you," said Val kindly.

"Who's got a sick dog?" I asked.

Friday, September 14, late at night

I sat in my room before the party and tried to figure out what I could say to Sondra.

"I'm sorry, Sondra, but I made a teeny-tiny change in your invitations. I hope you don't mind."

No, that wouldn't do.

"Hey, Sondra, guess what? I made a little mistake when I gave out the invitations."

No, she'd never fall for a lie like that.

And I couldn't tell her the truth. That would *never* do.

"Yo, Sondra—I decided your snobby A-list and B-list stuff was for the birds. So I changed a thing or two. Like it or lump it."

Forget it. She wouldn't like it. I might as well forget Sondra, I thought. I wasn't even sure why I still cared, but somehow I did. I couldn't help it.

I looked at my reflection in the mirror. I wanted to go to the party as Jellimiah. I'd have a better time.

But I *had* to talk to Missy and explain what had happened . . . so maybe I should go as John.

They couldn't both go to the same party, could they?

I thought.

Then I thought some more.

Then I got another one of my brainstorms. I grabbed that great black hat that Uncle Evan gave me, the one that's droopy and weird and covers my hair. It's the hair that makes changing back and forth so hard.

Then I remembered I had to at least start out as Jellimiah—he was the one who'd been invited to show up early.

"Goodness, John," said Mom when she saw me, "you're going to your first party at Edgewood in those ratty old clothes?"

"It's, um, a costume party, Mom," I said.

Mom looked me up and down. "Then what is it you're going as?"

"Um, I'm, well, I'm going as . . . as . . . well, what do *you* think I'm going as?"

Mom scrutinized me once again.

"Hmm," she said, "let's see. You could be a hobo. Or maybe a rock star."

"That's it," I said. "I'm a hobo rock star."

Mom shook her head. Then she smiled. "At least you're having fun," she said. "That's good. You're supposed to have fun at your age. You never seemed to have much fun back in Los Angeles. I think this move to New York's been a good change, don't you?"

"It certainly has been a change," I agreed.

"Why," continued Mom, "you're almost like a new person."

"Two new people," I said.

Mom looked puzzled.

"What I mean is, I'm, um, getting to know new people. That's it. That would change anybody."

Mom smiled again. "That's fine, dear. Have fun at your party. And remember to get home at a reasonable hour. And are you sure you have to bring your knapsack with you?"

"Yes, Mom, it goes where I go. See you later."

At Sondra's house a heavily made-up woman with bright blond hair and lots of jewelry answered the door. "So you're Jellimiah Jensen," she said. "My Sondra has told me all about you."

"Hey there, Mrs. Settle," I said, rearranging my hat.

"What a quaint hat," cooed Mrs. Settle.

"Thanks," I said. "I like it."

"So do I," came a voice from the stairs. It was Val. "Hi, Jellimiah. Glad you could get here early."

"Me too," I said. "Listen, Val, I've got to talk to Sondra about something. It's important."

"Sorry, no can do," said Mrs. Settle. "My Sondra's still having her hair done. I hired my hairdresser to come to the house especially. Unfortunately she got delayed, so Sondra won't be finished until right before the guests arrive. So you and Val can help me get the last things set out in the meantime."

"But I've got to talk to Sondra. I'll just go in while she's having her hair done."

"Now, now, Jellimiah," cooed Mrs. Settle, "no daughter of mine can be seen having her hair done."

"But—"

"It's all settled," said Mrs. Settle, sending Val and me into the living room to make sure the peanuts were in the little straw baskets.

"There is *so* much food!" gushed Val. "The A-list kids are going to eat like kings! Those B-list dorks will be lucky to get a few stale crumbs! There's enough food here tonight to feed the entire seventh grade!"

"That's kind of what I want to talk to Sondra about," I began, but Val had rushed into the dining room to add water to some vases.

"Tell me later!" she called behind her. "These roses need freshening up. I've heard aspirin works wonders!"

And Val darted off in search of aspirin.

I sat down in the living room to think.

"Well, young man," boomed a loud voice, "making yourself at home, I see."

I looked to my right and saw a pink-faced man in a gray suit.

"I'm Harrison K. Settle, Sondra's Dad," he told me.

"I'm Jellimiah J. Jensen," I replied, getting up and shaking his hand.

"So you're a classmate of Sondra's," he boomed jovially. I nodded. "Have you thought about what you're going to do when you finish college?"

I haven't gotten around to thinking about next year, much less what I'm doing after college. "No, not yet," I replied. "But I think my mom would like me to follow her in footsteps and go to medical school. She's a surgeon."

"Medical school? And expose yourself to all those malpractice suits? Did you know that doctors are sued more frequently than members of any other profession, and surgeons are sued most often of all? Why, just last March I sued the pants off some doctor right here in town. I . . ."

As Mr. Settle rambled on, I wondered idly if he would sue me for ruining Sondra's party.

At last Sondra appeared. Her hair was all swooped up on top of her head. I liked her better the other way, but she still looked pretty good, I guess.

"Sondra," I began, "there's something—"

But just then the doorbell rang.

"My first guest!" Sondra said excitedly, and raced over to answer the door.

With a triumphant smile, Sondra flung open the door. The smile fell from her lips when she saw who was standing there: Franklin Welch and his cousin Fred, the two biggest nerds in the seventh grade. And right behind them, running up the flagstone front walk and drooling a bit, came Regina Whitman, the biggest nerd-girl of all time. The light from the house was reflecting off her braces.

"Here I come—let's party!" she was squealing.

"Party! Party!" echoed Franklin and Fred.

Sondra had turned pale.

"What are *you* doing here?" she demanded, almost slamming the door in their faces.

All three waved their invitations.

Sondra grabbed them and read them.

"There's been a mistake. You got the wrong—" she began, but Regina, Franklin, and Fred waltzed past her and made a mad dash for the living room, where all three began stuffing peanuts into their mouths.

"How did those nerds get the wrong invitations?" Sondra murmured. Then she turned to me.

"Jellimiah," she said, "can I talk to you for a second?"

"Sure, man," I said, but I didn't get the chance. Just then in strode Whip and some of his football buddies.

"Hey Jellimiah!" said Whip, grabbing me by the shoulder and shoving me away from the front door. "Let me tell you all about practice . . . and then there's some other stuff."

By the time I'd heard about more touchdowns and interceptions than I could follow, the party was in full swing. I couldn't help but notice that about half the boys, as well as some of the girls, were dressed like Jellimiah!

I also noticed that Whip kept acting like he wanted to tell me something, but it never seemed to come out.

The Settle house was now overflowing with kids.

The entire seventh grade, in fact.

I'd invited everyone for the same night. I knew too well how it felt not to be invited to the best parties. Anyway, this whole party was supposed to pull the grade together, not divide it.

I looked around. Everyone was having a good time. No, not a good time—a *great* time. Nerds were talking to jocks, and brains were talking to the party crowd.

It would have been perfect if only Missy had been there. I still hoped she might show up—without Nick. I should have thrown *his* invitation in the trash!

Someone grabbed me from behind.

"Oh, Jellimiah," cooed a sweet voice. "I could just kiss you!"

And Sondra did.

"Whoa," I said, "what was that for?"

"You sneaky dog," cooed Sondra. "I know it was you who invited the entire class. At first I wanted to kill you, but look—it's turned out to be the best party ever! Like, *everyone's* come up to me and said, like, it was so cool I'd invited everyone! Even Jake said I was way cool! You know, *I* wanted to invite everyone, but my mother said I couldn't. She said it would, like, ruin my reputation. So I'm glad *you* did. Thank you!"

And she kissed me again.

Then she whirled off to get some more soda.

So Sondra didn't hate me for what I had done. It kind of made me think about staying Jellimiah after all!

Then I saw the front door open and in walked Missy and Nick. I made a mad dash for the bathroom.

"John!" cried Missy when I found her and Nick a bit later by the food table. "I was looking for you, but I didn't see you or your brother. Is Jellimiah here, too?"

"Sure," I said. "We're both here."

"Listen," said Missy, a serious look coming into her brown eyes, "I have an apology to make. Mr. Forester talked to Nick and me about your story. I'm sorry I ever thought you'd steal your brother's story."

"That's okay," I said. "It's just one of the drawbacks of having a twin. These mistakes happen."

"Well, it's one heck of a good story," said Nick with a friendly smile. "You're one good writer.'"

"Thanks," I said modestly. But inside I felt like yelling, "Yes!"

"Do you want to dance?" asked a nervous voice from behind me.

"Gosh, Cindi," I said, turning around, "I'm a terrible dancer. Really terrible."

Cindi's face fell. Instantly I realized that even though I'd told the truth, she thought I was just saying that not to dance with her. Cindi's not the most popular girl in the world.

"But I know someone who will," I said. "My brother. He likes to dance."

I don't even know why I said it. But dancing just seemed like something Jellimiah would like to do.

"Jellimiah would dance with me?" gasped Cindi.

"Sure," I said. "Just wait here. I'll go get him."

"Let's go," I said three minutes later, my hat in place and my ragged clothes back on. A second later Cindi and I were leaping all around the dance floor. Cindi was a surprisingly good dancer. So was I. And I never even knew I could dance. I've always been too shy to really let loose before. But not anymore.

"Wow," said Sondra when the song was over, "you and Cindi really put everyone else on the dance floor to shame."

I beamed, and Cindi blushed. It must have been the first time Sondra had ever complimented Cindi.

"My turn now," said Sondra.

She didn't dance quite as well as Cindi. But I was dancing with Sondra Settle, the most popular girl in the seventh grade! Me, who back in Los Angeles didn't even get invited to the cool parties! Being Jellimiah sure has its benefits!

After that song Sondra and I rejoined Missy, Nick, and Cindi. I noticed Jake and Regina chatting by the potato chips. And Whip was talking to Albert by the onion dip!

When the deejay put on another good dance tune, Missy looked around hopefully.

"Hey," I said, "would you like to dance?"

Missy looked embarrassed.

"Sorry, Jellimiah," she said, "but I was kind of looking for John."

"He doesn't like dancing," Cindi piped up.

"Oh," said Missy, all disappointed.

"Well," I said, "it's time he did. I'll go talk him into it."

Three minutes later John appeared. I took Missy by the hand and said, "May I have this dance?"

"You bet," said Missy with a grin. Nick didn't seem to mind. I guess he's not the jealous type.

Missy danced as well as Cindi. And John danced as well as Jellimiah. Maybe even better. I couldn't believe it. I never knew I could do this!

"Wow!" said Missy breathlessly, "you dance as well as you write."

"Thanks," I said. I felt like I could stay John for ever and ever!

"But do you and your brother always wear backpacks when you dance?" she added.

I smiled and pretended I couldn't hear her over the music.

We were relaxing by the cold cuts later when Whip came over. "Hey, John," he said, "I've been looking for Jellimiah."

"Uh, I can go get him," I said.

"Thanks," said Whip, "but I've gotta go—I've got a practice early tomorrow. Can you tell Jellimiah I was looking for him?"

"Sure. But about practice tomorrow . . . well, his ligament—"

"I'm glad to see it's all healed," Whip interrupted.

"It is?" I said.

"Yeah," Whip said. "No one can dance like that with a sprained ligament. Jellimiah must have heard from the doctor it was all right, huh?"

"The doctor?" I said.

"Yeah, Jellimiah told me he was taking you to the doctor this afternoon. I guess he got checked out, too."

"Uh . . . yes," I said. *Uh-oh,* I thought. *I've got to find a way to get out of football practice. Maybe this means I'll have to stay John after all.* "Listen, Whip," I said, "I'm, um, not sure Jellimiah can come tomorrow. He's, I mean, we, we're, um, helping my mom with some stuff."

"Then can you have him call me?" asked Whip.

"Sure," I said with a sinking feeling.

Whip looked serious.

"Listen, John," he said, "maybe it would be better coming from you, being Jellimiah's twin and all. I didn't have the heart to tell him before, but it's like this: Everyone from the team last year wants to come back, so it's a rule they get first dibs. There just isn't any room on the team for Jellimiah. I'm sorry."

"I'll break it to him," I said, working hard not to laugh with relief.

"Thanks, buddy," said Whip. "I hope Jellimiah takes it as well."

As he left I thought, *Now I can stay Jellimiah if I want to!* John or Jellimiah, Jellimiah or John . . .

I spent the rest of the night going back and forth between the two. And not just in my head. It was a good thing the Settle house was so big—I'd found a little bathroom on the second floor that no one else seemed to use, and I changed there.

So when I was John, I danced with Missy. Then when I was Jellimiah, I danced with Sondra. And once in a while I danced with Cindi.

It got confusing, but it was fun. A lot of fun.

And I got away with it.

But why not? If Superman could confuse Metropolis with that Clark Kent bit all those years, why shouldn't I confuse Edgewood with my John/Jellimiah bit for a week and a half?

A little while later I was taking a much-needed break from dancing. Standing by the snack table, the party going on full swing behind me, I was trying to decide between a chocolate brownie and a lemon square when I felt someone staring at me.

It was Albert.

"Hey, Albert," I said, "which would you choose—the brownie or the lemon square?"

Albert stared right into my eyes, down deep.

"That's not hard," he said in his clipped voice.

"It is," I argued. "I don't know which to choose."

Albert smiled.

"You don't have to choose," he said.

"What do you mean?" I asked.

"I mean," said Albert, "that you can have both if you want to. You can choose both, Jensen. It's all up to you."

～

Monday, September 17, fourth period

I got up early this morning.

I had a lot to think about.

Today I had to choose who I was going to be.

And I guess because my time as twins is over, today is also going to be the last time I write in this journal.

I sat on my bed and sighed.

To distract myself, I decided to figure out how I'd get rid of whoever it was I was going to get rid of.

First I thought about saying he'd been run over by a truck. I started imagining all the sympathy I'd get if people believed my twin had been squashed flatter than a pancake!

But then I realized that if one of us died, people would send condolence notes to Mom. And they'd expect to have heard reports about it on the news: "Teen Flattened in Tragic Mishap"—that sort of thing.

Then I thought about saying one of us had run away.

But if it was Jellimiah, Sondra would probably have her dad pay for a detective to go look for him. And if it was John, Miss Thompson might do the same thing!

Next I thought that if I decided to get rid of Jellimiah, I could say he'd been arrested and sent to jail forever and ever. But they don't send seventh-graders to jail.

After that I thought that if I got rid of John, I could say he'd won a scholarship to a school for super-smart brain types. That would impress Missy. But then what would it matter? John wouldn't be around anymore for Missy to show him how impressed she was.

"You look preoccupied, dear," said Mom over breakfast.

"I'm trying to figure something out," I replied, playing with my cereal.

"Is it something you'd like to talk about?" asked Mom.

"Um, I don't think so," I answered. I know that sooner or later, Mom will hear about my little scam. I just hope it'll be later. My plan is to bring up the topic gradually, then eventually tell Mom all about it. Maybe around Christmas. Mom loves Christmas. She's always in a good mood then. That's when I'll tell her . . . I think.

Mom took a sip of coffee and smiled.

"John," she said in her serious voice, "I am so proud of you. I know moving is hard on a teenager, but you've handled it beautifully. You seem much more sure of yourself—more outgoing, too. There's nothing you can't do."

Except be two people at one time, I thought.

Breakfast was over and I still hadn't made up my mind about who I was going to be.

I was still trying to decide when I headed off for school.

From force of habit I was wearing my John clothes—ironed shirt, pressed pants, black shoes. My hair was neatly combed. But dressing like this seemed as much of a costume as dressing like Jellimiah.

John or Jellimiah . . . Jellimiah or John.

I walked to school. But slowly. Very slowly.

John or Jellimiah . . . Jellimiah or John.

Who should I be?

Who?

I kept on walking, slower and slower. When I got to the woods surrounding Edgewood Junior High, I stopped altogether. I sat down on a fallen tree and thought.

I was still thinking when I heard the bell ring at eight-thirty.

But I didn't care.

I could be late once in a while if I felt like it.

When the late bell rang five minutes later, it was like a bell ringing right inside my head.

I had it figured out—all of it.

I thought it through again, just to be sure, and it still sounded good to me. Very good.

I had one or two things to get ready before I went to school, but it didn't take long.

"Thank goodness you're here!" cried Ms. Betterton when I arrived at school. "We were so worried you might be absent again! And where's your brother?"

"I'm the only one here now," I said mysteriously.

Ms. Betterton looked me up and down. She seemed a bit baffled.

"I don't know," she said, half to herself, "but I could *never* tell you two apart—you look alike as two peas in a pod to me." She examined me again, head to toe. "And which one are you?" she asked.

I smiled again—mysteriously. But I said nothing.

"Oh, well," said Ms. Betterton, "never mind about that now. Just hurry along into the auditorium."

"The auditorium?" I asked.

"Thank heaven at least one of you two showed up," continued Ms. Betterton, directing me down the hall toward the stage door to the auditorium. "Missy and her cousin can conduct the interview afterward, instead of before, the way they wanted to."

"Who's Missy's cousin?" I asked as Ms. Betterton opened the door and practically shoved me through.

"Why, Nick Clarke. They're just as close as brother and sister. Now, here we go!"

Cousins! I was so happy to hear that Missy *wasn't* going out with Nick that suddenly I was tempted to change my plan. It wasn't too late.

But I decided to stick to my original idea. I knew it was the right choice.

"Good luck!" cried Ms. Betterton as she pushed me forward—right onto the stage of the auditorium.

"What's going on?" I gasped as a thunderous roar of applause almost ripped the room apart.

The entire junior high was there, applauding me!

But why?

My decision hadn't been *that* breathtaking, I thought. And besides, no one even knew I was going to be making it.

Clip-clop, clip-clop sounded from across the stage.

Miss Thompson was trotting toward me, a smile on her face. A real smile, too. When she reached me, she gave me an enormous hug. I thought I would die.

Then she turned toward the audience and began speaking.

"People," she said, "the boy you see on the stage beside me has, as I believe some of you know by now, done a

147

foolhardy yet very, very brave thing. With only his twin brother to assist him, he captured the burglars who'd been steadily stripping Edgewood of both its electronic equipment and, perhaps more important, its sense of security. But thanks to our newest student, that is all behind us."

The auditorium erupted in applause again.

"In addition," continued Miss Thompson, "he has also alerted me to two other, uh, situations." Here she paused and stared hard at Mr. Fishwell and then at Mr. Trotter. "I believe these two situations have been resolved satisfactorily."

Once more applause sounded.

"Now," Miss Thompson went on as I stood there dazed, "it is my pleasure to present this certificate of appreciation from Edgewood Junior High and the town of Edgewood."

"Speech! Speech!" cried some of the students from their seats.

"Yes," said Miss Thompson, handing me the certificate, "perhaps we could hear a few words from . . . from . . ."

The principal looked at me quizzically.

"Which one are you?" she whispered.

She'd whispered it, but as she was standing so near the microphone, everyone heard her. And everyone started staring at me all the harder.

Yes, I was still wearing my John clothes. My shirt was ironed and clean. And my pants were pressed. But my shirt wasn't buttoned up to the top, and my pants had huge rips in them. Yes, I was still wearing my black John shoes—but they were all scuffed up and muddy from my stroll through the woods. And while my hair wasn't moussed, it wasn't all combed and neat, either. It was wild and tousled. On my face was a smile that was part Jellimiah smirk and part John grin.

I could see confusion in everyone's face.

"You're John, aren't you?" said Miss Thompson, looking into my eyes. "I can tell by your sweet expression."

"No such luck," I heard Mr. Fishwell grumble from the side of the auditorium. "It's Jellimiah. I can tell by the look on his face."

"I only wish it were," disagreed Mr. Trotter unhappily. "It looks like John to me—that little sneak."

"It has to be Jellimiah," said Sondra to Val from her seat in the front row. "He looks way too cool to be John."

"Way cool," replied Val in a way that told me she couldn't tell which twin I was.

"I think it's John," disagreed Whip, who was sitting on Sondra's left. "Jellimiah is more athletic-looking."

"Nah," countered Jake. "I agree with Sondra. It's Jellimiah. He's got kind of a smirk. And his pants are all ripped."

"But his shirt is ironed," Cindi noted, staring hard at me from Jake's right. "I say it's John."

The rumble of people trying to figure out who I was was growing louder. It was a good thing my friends were all sitting in the front row, otherwise I'd never have been able to hear what they were saying.

Nick was examining me carefully. He even took off his glasses, cleaned them, and put them back on. But he still looked baffled. Now that I knew he was only Missy's cousin, I decided he could think whatever he felt like thinking!

"I lean toward John," he said thoughtfully. "But it could be Jellimiah."

Missy was staring at me, a bright light in her brown eyes.

"It's John," she said with a smile. "I can tell by the way he's smiling at me."

Then she blushed.

I blushed, too. I realized I had been smiling at her. Not at Sondra, but at Missy.

Only Albert kept his mouth shut. But he grinned at me. Then he gave me a thumbs-up sign. Then he put up his other hand, too—*two* thumbs-up signs. So at least *he* knew. Something tells me he's known all along. After all, he's a real twin. And something also tells me I've found a friend. I flashed two thumbs-up signs back at him. I mean, he's the one who gave me the hint about choosing who I'd be.

At last Miss Thompson silenced the auditorium.

"John—it is John, isn't it?" she said uncertainly. "Would you care to say a few words?"

"It's Jellimiah," grumbled Mr. Fishwell again.

I stepped forward, and once again the room exploded in applause.

I raised my hands and silenced the auditorium.

Then I leaned forward and spoke in the microphone—loudly and clearly and proudly. Me. All alone. In front of the entire school.

"Thank you for your applause," I said. "And for the certificate. I'm just glad it turned out so well. On behalf of my brother, let me say thank you again. Now I have some news for you: my brother has moved back to California, to be with our dad. He left yesterday. So from now on, there will be only one Jensen boy in the seventh grade."

"Yeah, but which one are you?" called out Jake.

I bowed my head. Then I raised it and continued speaking.

"I've got a new name," I said. "From now on you can call me J.J."

"That stands for Jellimiah Jensen," I heard Sondra informing Val. "I like it, too. The name Jellimiah never worked for me. It was major uncool. But J.J.—that's totally buff."

"J.J.," I heard Missy repeating. "For John Jensen. I like it," she told her cousin. "He never seemed like a John to me. I'm going to like calling him J.J."

Yes, I thought, *J.J. is me.* I'm not just Jellimiah for my grandfather anymore. And I'm not just John for my father. I'm someone new. I'm J.J.

"Well, uh, J.J.," said Miss Thompson, "thank you."

I could tell she was still trying to decide who I was. I know that sooner or later I'll have to become John or Jellimiah officially, but that doesn't really matter. What's in a name, anyway? What really matters is that I've become the best of both. I can be a good student. I can be wild. I can speak in front of big groups. I can even dance. And something tells me I won't be eating lunch alone ever again.

I did it.

And I'm only beginning!

Yes!